"I'm Ms. Schonberg's lawyer," the guy said. "She left something to Ella in her will."

"Well, that's great news," Dad said. "How nice of Golda to think of you, Ella! We'll certainly be at the will reading to find out all about it."

"No, no," the man said quickly. "I have it here."

Guess it's not a piano, I thought.

The lawyer leaned into the backseat of his car and pulled out a square black bag with a long strap and a little handle on top.

"What —?" I started to say, reaching for it.

And then, all of a sudden . . . the bag moved.

Get into some

Pet Trouble

Runaway Retriever

Loudest Beagle on the Block

Mud-Puddle Poodle

Pet Trouble

Loudest Beagle on the Block

by T.T. SUTHERLAND

SCHOLASTIC INC.

New York   Toronto   London   Auckland   Sydney
Mexico City   New Delhi   Hong Kong   Buenos Aires

"Leader of the Pack"
Words and Music by George Morton, Jeff Barry, and Ellie Greenwich
© 1964 (Renewed 1992) SCREEN GEMS-EMI MUSIC INC.
and TENDER TUNES MUSIC CO.
All Rights Controlled and Administered by
SCREEN GEMS-EMI MUSIC INC.
All Rights Reserved   International Copyright Secured   Used by Permission

ISBN-13: 978-0-545-10242-1
ISBN-10: 0-545-10242-1

12 11 10 9 8 7 6 5 4 3 2   9 10 11 12 13 14/0

Printed in the U.S.A.
First printing, April 2009

For Emma and Olivia — TTS

CHAPTER 1

You might think that any story that starts with a dog at a funeral would either be sad or scary — like maybe it turns out it's actually a zombie dog that wants to eat your brains. But this story isn't about a zombie dog. Trumpet could be a pretty bad dog, but at least she just eats dog food. We got her in a cemetery, but she is definitely alive and not some spooky night creature.

So it's true this story begins with a funeral, but I promise it isn't scary or sad.

The story, I mean. I guess funerals are always sad. But Great-Aunt Golda was like 106 years old or something. I'm not even kidding. She was really old. Mom said, "It was her time," and Dad said, "She lived a good long life," which was true. Great-Aunt Golda used to be a famous opera singer. She traveled all over the world singing opera everywhere. I hope I get to be that famous one day — I want to be a Broadway star, and then sing in Sydney and Paris and Milan and anywhere they'll let me onto the stage!

I didn't know Great-Aunt Golda very well. What I remember about her is that she wore a lot of silk scarves in different shades of red, and she smelled like coconuts and challah bread. She was also pretty big — as big as my mom and dad put together — and she talked in this big, dramatic voice like she was about to start singing at any moment. Like she was full of opera and it might just spill out all of a sudden.

"Ella!" she would cry whenever Mom brought me over. "Ella, my darling! You need some meat on those bones! A truly great singer needs a lot of *oomph* behind her!" She would bring her fists forward to emphasize the "oomph." Then she would take my shoulders and steer me over to the piano. Red silk scarves wrapped around my arms and face as she hugged me. I imagine that's what it feels like to be mummified, at least if your tomb is also full of coconuts. "Now sing for me, darling! Sing!" she'd bellow, flinging one hand dramatically in the air.

I would play all of her favorite classical music and she would sit in her big yellow paisley armchair, tapping along on the cushions and smiling. Sometimes she would shake her curly, dark-red hair and go, "A marvel! A gift from God, this one is!" She always dyed her hair, so that's one reason I never knew how old she was. Plus she had a "big presence," as Mom always said.

I also didn't know she had a dog. But I sure found that out.

It was a few days before I started sixth grade. I was playing the piano, like I usually am, when Mom came in to tell me that Great-Aunt Golda had died in her sleep.

"Oh, no," I said. "Poor Aunt Golda." I felt guilty. "I didn't even see her this summer. I haven't sung for her in ages."

"It's all right, Ella — she knew how busy you were with your music," Mom said. "She always said how important that was."

That was true. But sometimes she would also shake her curls at me and say: "I hope you are still living your life, my darling! I hope you live every day to its utmost! Engage the world! Experience everything you can! Live! Live!" Whatever that means.

I'd say, "Yes, Aunt Golda, I will. I mean, I do."

"Such a serious one," she'd say, pinching my cheek.

"She wanted you to sing at her funeral," Mom said. "Would you do that?"

"Of course!" I said.

I love to sing, and I especially love to sing in public — that's, like, the *only* thing I like to do in public! Otherwise I'm pretty shy. I know music is the one thing I'm good at, so I like performing. I'd never sung at a funeral before. What if I wasn't sad enough? What if her ghost didn't like it? I was also scared that I'd have to learn some kind of funeral song in Hebrew, but Mom said I could do something I already knew.

In the end we chose a song called "Time to Say Goodbye." I have a version that Sarah Brightman sings which is *a-mazing*. I totally love her. I know that makes me weird, that my favorite music is classical and opera and Broadway show tunes. I know I should love Rihanna and Miley Cyrus instead. But I figure one day when I go off to music school I'll finally meet other people who like the same things I do, so why should I change what I like?

The funeral was on the Saturday before school started. It was already kind of a gray, misty day when I got up in the morning. Mom let me wear my black velvet dress, which I like because it makes me feel like I'm a grown-up performing at Carnegie Hall or something. It has short sleeves and the same kind of soft glow that a piano does. My mom combed and combed my dark brown hair, trying to get it straight, but my curls are hard to fight. Golda always let her curls go crazy, so I figured she wouldn't mind if my hair wasn't exactly perfect. Mom wanted to tie my braids with gold ribbons, to bring out the gold flecks in my brown eyes, but I picked red ones instead, in honor of Golda's silk scarves.

I sat at the piano and warmed up my voice while everyone else was getting ready.

"La la la la la la la la la," I sang, running the scales on the piano. It always calms me down when I sit on my piano bench and touch the smooth white keys. I love my piano the way some girls love jewelry or shoes. It makes me feel pretty and sophisticated.

"LA LA LA LA LA LA LA LA LAAAAAA!" my little brother, Isaac, shouted from the next room.

"Mom!" I yelled, but not too loud so I wouldn't strain my voice. "Isaac is interrupting my practice again!"

Isaac stuck his head around the door. "Tattletale," he said, sticking out his tongue. Isaac is only two years younger than me — he's in fourth grade — but I swear he acts like he's still five years old. Mom says I should be patient and set a mature example. I *try* to do that, but seriously, he is *so annoying*. I'm sure Sarah Brightman and Charlotte Church don't have annoying little brothers hollering at them while they're rehearsing.

Mom came and marched Isaac off to try to wash his face, which always looks like it's covered in chocolate, even first thing in the morning. Then we all had to hurry into the car and rush to the temple. Mom drove so Dad could look at his notes. He was as nervous as I was, because he was supposed to get up and give a "eulogy," which is like a big speech about Great-Aunt Golda's life and how long and special it was. And he had to go first, because the eulogy would be at the temple service, and I didn't have to sing until we got to the cemetery.

He didn't have to worry, though. Dad works in sales at this technology company, so he's a total whiz at presenting and giving speeches. He loves an audience. He used to be in his own rock band, actually. They weren't very good, but don't tell him that! They were called The Smashing Mozarts. That's how he met Mom — she was doing a graduate thesis on Mozart and saw a poster with the band name on it, so she went to one of his shows.

He thought she was "radical" and a "babe." She thought their music was "atonal" and "absolutely horrifying." She wouldn't return any of his first thirty calls, but eventually he won her over. Like I said, he's a good salesman.

His speech was about how Great-Aunt Golda wasn't afraid of anything. He told the story of how she got herself out of Poland in the 1940s. He talked about how she once met President John F. Kennedy, which is a story we've all heard lots of times, but everyone applauded and laughed. He talked about how her music was her life, but she always made time for her friends and family and having adventures. And then at the end he played a record of her singing, which made me nervous, because how was I supposed to follow a big opera star like that?

I had to hope that everyone would forget how good she sounded while they were driving from the temple to the cemetery. I poked Isaac, who was totally falling asleep in his chair. In another minute, he'd be keeling over into my lap and probably drooling on my nice dress.

"Wake up!" I whispered. The music was loud enough to hide my voice, but Mom frowned at me anyway. At me! When Isaac was the one being bad. He blinked and rubbed his eyes and kind of kicked the air a few times. But at least he didn't nod off again.

Finally we all went outside and got in our cars so we could follow the long black hearse to the cemetery. I thought it would be rude to sing on the way there, especially with Nana and Pop-Pop in the car with us (that's Mom's parents — Pop-Pop is Great-Aunt Golda's brother, if you want to know all that). So I just hummed under my breath, trying to warm up my voice.

As we got out of the car at the cemetery, I smoothed down my velvet dress, going over the words in my mind. Mom motioned for me to go up in front of everyone — all my aunts and cousins and uncles and a lot of old people in bright colors who were probably Golda's theater friends. I whispered, "I hope you like this song, Aunt Golda. I know you would have sung it better."

Then I turned and faced the crowd of people standing around the coffin. I tried to pretend that I was onstage, and that their faces were all bright stage lights instead of eyes staring at me. I looked over their heads and saw a new silver car pull up behind ours. A guy in a suit with a pink tie got out. He looked sweaty and kind of flustered.

I closed my eyes to block him out and started singing. Once the music is in my head, everything else falls away. Singing makes me feel like I'm flying, especially when it's something really slow and sweet and beautiful, like this song.

The last few notes drifted away. I stood there for a moment, feeling like my feet were coming back down to earth. Then everyone started clapping. Mom had tears in her eyes. I hoped that meant Great-Aunt Golda would have liked it, too.

There were a few more words and the burial, and then we all started to head back to our cars. Aunts and uncles kept stopping us to tell me they loved my voice. Kooky Aunt Miriam said that maybe I was Golda reincarnated, which didn't make any sense, because I'd already been alive at the same time as her for eleven years. But Mom and I smiled politely and said thank you, because we knew she meant it nicely.

I noticed that the suit guy was kind of hovering around our car like he was waiting for us. I know we have a lot of family, but I was pretty sure I hadn't ever seen him before. Was he an old friend of Golda's? I couldn't figure out why he just stayed at the back the whole time, or why he only came to the cemetery part.

At last we managed to say good-bye to everyone and get back to our car. Then the suit guy hurried forward. He pulled out a white silk handkerchief and wiped his face. It wasn't hot or anything, but he was sweating anyway. Actually, it was starting to rain. Mom went past him and opened the trunk to get out the umbrellas for us. I knew Isaac and I would have to share an umbrella, which was annoying because he always hogs the whole thing and half of me ends up getting soaked.

So at this critical life-changing moment, I was thinking about umbrellas and my nice dress getting wet and stupid Isaac. I wasn't thinking about dogs at all.

Then the suit guy looked at me and said, "Are you Ella Finegold?"

Well, you could have knocked me over with a pancake, as Golda would have said. "Yeah," I said.

"I'm Ella's father," Dad said, putting one hand on my shoulder. "Who are you?"

The guy looked relieved. "I'm Ms. Schonberg's lawyer," he said. It took me a minute to figure out he meant Golda. "She left something to Ella in her will."

That made all of us relax right away. I couldn't believe it! Great-Aunt Golda was so cool. What had she left me? Maybe it was her collection of old records. Or her piano! It had to be something musical. She had some old songbooks that would be amazing to own. I hadn't even thought about getting anything from her before.

Dad smiled, taking and opening the umbrella Mom was handing to him. "Well, that's great news," he said. "How nice of Golda to think of you, Ella! We'll certainly be at the will reading to find out all about it."

"No, no," the man said quickly. "I mean, yes, you should be there, but I'm afraid you need to take this gift right now. I have it here."

Mom and I gave each other puzzled looks. *Guess it's not a piano,* I thought.

"Here? Now?" Mom said. "Isn't this a bit irregular?"

"I can't keep it another day," the man said, wiping his forehead again. He started hurrying back to his car and we all followed him. I tried to take the umbrella from Isaac so I could hold it, but he wrestled it away from me. Big fat raindrops splatted on my carefully braided hair and pretty dress.

The lawyer leaned into the backseat of his car and pulled out a square black bag with a long strap and a little handle on top. One end of the bag was mesh and the top roof had a big U-shaped zipper.

"What —?" I started to say, reaching for it.

And then, all of a sudden . . . the bag moved.

CHAPTER 2

"**I**T'S ALIIIIIIIIIIIIVE!" Isaac yelled at the top of his lungs, like a swamp creature had popped out of the ground or something. And by the way, if you're wondering, this is not the best thing to yell in a cemetery. I saw people at a funeral halfway up the next hill all turn around to stare at us.

The bag wriggled like crazy in the lawyer's hands. I jumped back. "It *is* alive!" I squeaked.

"What on earth is in there?" Mom demanded. Dad leaned down and peeked inside.

"AROOOOOOOOOOOOOOOOOOOOOOOOO-OOOOOOOOOOO!" went the bag. It was the loudest howl I'd ever heard. Seriously, the people at the other funeral must have thought the whole place was haunted. I practically wanted to run away myself.

"Oh, wow," Dad said. "Ella, look."

At a ghost in a bag? No thanks. But I couldn't really say no to Dad, so I edged closer and peeked through the mesh.

A pair of enormous brown eyes met mine. Two white paws were pressed up to the screen.

"It's a dog!" I gasped.

"Awwrrrooo," the bag said sadly. The dog poked its wet black nose at me and scratched the mesh screen with its claws.

"I didn't know Aunt Golda had a dog," my mom said, looking confused. "Why would she leave it to Ella?"

The lawyer pressed his handkerchief to his forehead again. "She didn't have it very long," he said. "It's not much more than a puppy — about a year old, the vet guessed. I have all its paperwork here." He dumped the bag in my hands and reached into his car.

I don't know what the dog was doing in there, but the bag flailed and jumped so much that I nearly dropped it on the ground. I had to wrap my arms around it to keep it still.

"All its vaccinations," the lawyer said, handing my dad a manila envelope. He was talking faster and faster, like a horse speeding up when it sees the finish line. "It's up-to-date, spayed, housebroken, healthy, here's some food, a leash, good luck, nice meeting you —"

"Wait, wait," Dad said, juggling the things that

were being shoved into his hands. "We've never had a dog — we're not exactly equipped — this is so —"

"Well, she left it to you," the lawyer said. "You can do with it what you like, but I suggest waiting to hear the details of the will before you make any decisions. I'll see you Thursday at the reading." He backed away in a hurry, nodding and kind of bowing to us. Before Dad could say anything else, the lawyer leaped back into his car and drove away.

That's when I noticed how drenched I was. Isaac had totally forgotten about holding up the umbrella. He was jumping around, trying to look inside the dog carrier.

"AWWWWWRRRRRRRRRROOOOOOOO-OOOOOOOOOO," the dog went again.

"Oh, dear," my mom said. "Henry, now what do we do?"

"I guess we take it home with us," Dad said. "Come on, let's get out of the rain. We'll take a better look at it in the car."

We all ran back to our car. I was still holding the dog carrier in my arms. The mesh side was tilted up toward my face and I could see the dog inside scrabbling around and looking up at me.

Maybe I should stop and explain something. I'm OK with dogs. I don't love them and I don't hate them. Aunt Miriam has a fat little Pekingese named Desperado, who comes with her whenever we host Thanksgiving or Rosh Hashanah. Desperado might be the mellowest animal on the planet. As soon as he gets to our house, he waddles over to the couch. He's too short and fat to jump up himself, so he stands there and waits until Aunt Miriam picks him up and puts him on a pillow. And then he falls asleep for the rest of the night. Seriously, I've never heard him make a single noise. Once she forgot to put him up on the couch and an hour later he was still just standing there, waiting for her to remember.

So I kind of figured that dogs were nothing to get excited about. Heidi Tyler, who's in my class at school, talks about dogs practically nonstop. She loves them and she wants one so badly, but her mom and dad always say no because their house is too neat for a dog. It's true. I went there once for a party a couple of years ago. (I don't go to a lot of parties because I usually have piano lessons or choir practice or something — I always put my music first. I figure one day I'll be famous and then I'll have lots of time to make friends.) I think Heidi's mom made her invite all the girls in fourth grade. Their house is scary neat. Most of the furniture is white and there are hundreds of small breakable things everywhere. It *is* too neat for a dog.

Actually, it's even too neat for Heidi. I'm not sure how she gets from the front door to her room without messing stuff up.

My mom thinks that being too neat is a sign that you're not letting yourself be creative. She says her messy office is a sign of a busy mind at work. But her mess doesn't have pets in it. Mom has never had a pet in her life. A few years ago, Dad said maybe we should get a dog. He had a dog when he was a kid, a long time ago. But Mom said she would have to do all the work taking care of it, and Isaac and I didn't get too excited about it, so he dropped the idea.

I do have a goldfish. Its name is Bird. That's the kind of joke I thought was funny when I got it in first grade. It doesn't sound quite so funny when I tell people nowadays, but I don't have friends over very often, so it doesn't come up much. I feed him and clean his bowl once a week and he just kind of floats around looking bored. That's sort of what I thought all pets were like.

Until I met this dog.

We all jumped into our car and shook ourselves off. I dumped the dog carrier on the seat between me and Isaac. I squeezed my braids and water dripped out of them. Rain splattered on the roof and on the windshield. It sounded like the percussion section of an orchestra practicing outside, especially when the thunder joined in, *BOOM BOOOOOOM!*

Mom fluffed out her hair and dried off her glasses, and then she turned around to peer into the backseat. "My goodness," she said. "I guess we should let it out and say hello. Henry, does it have a name?"

My dad opened the manila envelope. He squinted at the pages inside. "This says it's a she," he said. "And her name is Trumpet."

"Trumpet?" I repeated, wrinkling my nose. Trumpets aren't my favorite instrument. They're too loud and brassy. I like pretty, quiet instruments, like the harp and the piano and the flute. "That's a weird name for a dog," I said. "Especially a girl dog. I'd call her Piccolo or Viola instead."

"Maybe she's a Miles Davis fan," Dad said.

"Who's that?" Isaac said.

Dad clutched his heart. "What are they teaching our children these days?" he asked my mom in a big tragic voice.

"He's a jazz guy, a trumpeter," I said to Isaac, and my little brother lost interest right away. He didn't get any of the musical genes in the family. Which is only one of the many reasons I think maybe Mom and

Dad found him on the doorstep or something. There's no way we could be related. I could never be as loud and irritating as he is.

"Well, let's let her out," Mom said. Dad twisted around. His eyes were kind of twinkly. He actually looked excited.

I took the zipper at the top of the bag and pulled it slowly, unzipping the big U. Before I'd gotten it open very far, a shiny black nose appeared in the opening. The dog poked and wriggled like she thought she could fit her whole body out through that tiny hole if she just tried hard enough. I pulled the zipper the rest of the way and the top of the bag peeled back.

An explosion of fur flew out of the bag. Before I could even blink, a white and brown blur leaped onto my dress and tried to climb up onto my shoulders. Its paws caught in my hair and pulled one of my ribbons loose. I shrieked as the dog started licking my face with a big, pink, surprisingly scratchy tongue.

"Awww, she likes you!" Dad said, clearly not seeing the difference between "liking me" and "trampling me into the car seat."

I was too busy trying to protect my face with my arms to answer him. The dog was practically up on my shoulders, poking its nose into every gap, trying everything it could do to get past my hands so it could lick my face again. Its whole body was wriggling so hard that I thought it would knock itself onto the floor of the car.

"See, look how she's wagging her tail," Dad said. He reached over the seat to scratch the dog's head. Trumpet jumped at his hand. Her claws dug into my legs as she pushed herself up. Her ears flapped around and she started to make this funny squeaking sound.

"What is that?" Isaac said. "What's that noise?"

"It's just how she says hi," Dad said. He let the dog sniff his hand all over, which made her be still long enough for us to look at her.

Trumpet was bigger than Aunt Miriam's Pekingese, but she wasn't very big. Her legs were long and white with big white paws at the end like fat marshmallows. Her back and head and ears were a soft tan color, like a cello or a new violin, with a patch of black in the middle of her back. Her long straight tail had a white spot right at the tip, and there was a triangle of white running down from a spot on her forehead, between her brown eyes, and over her whole muzzle. Her chest and underbelly were white, too. Her ears were long and droopy and smooth. They looked as silky as my velvet dress.

"She *is* pretty," Mom said as if she was looking for something nice to say.

"Of course she is. She's a beagle," Dad said. "Hey there Trumpet. How's it going, girl?" He scratched behind her floppy ears and her tail started going like a motor.

"A beagle?" I said. "I thought Snoopy on *Charlie Brown* was a beagle."

"That's true," Dad said.

"But he's black and white," I said. "He doesn't look like Trumpet, except maybe for the ears."

"You'll have to take that up with the cartoonist," Dad said jokingly. "Aww, look at her licking my hands. Do I taste like chicken, Trumpet?" She wagged her tail and gazed up at him with her big soft eyes.

Mom looked worried. "Don't get attached, Henry," she said. "We have to talk about this."

"All right," Dad said with a sigh. He gave Trumpet one last scratch behind her ears and then turned around again. He started the car. "We'll take her home for now and figure out the next step tomorrow."

"I like her!" Isaac announced.

"That's because she hasn't tried to lick your face off yet," I said. I glanced down at my dress. It was covered in little white and brown hairs. As the car started to move, before I could stop her, Trumpet curled up on my lap. She rolled onto her back like she was offering her belly to me. Her ears flipped up so I could see their pink-and-white undersides. She kind of looked like she was smiling.

"She wants you to rub her tummy," Isaac said. He reached over the bag and patted Trumpet's stomach.

"Are you sure? That's weird," I said.

"Isaac's right. Dogs like that," Dad said, peeking at us in the rearview mirror.

I gingerly touched Trumpet's pink-and-white stomach. It was much softer than I expected. I ran my fingers through the little whorls of short white fur. She wagged her tail and wriggled closer to me, resting her head on my free arm.

OK, I thought. *Maybe she is a little bit cute.*

But I knew there had to be a catch. Why had the lawyer been so eager to get rid of her? Why had he rushed away in such a hurry? If she was a good dog, why didn't he want to keep her even a minute longer?

I had a feeling there was something we didn't know yet about Trumpet.

CHAPTER 3

When we got home, I led Trumpet over to the couch. She seemed confused, so I picked her up, just like Desperado, and put her down on one of the pillows. But instead of lying down, she turned in a circle, and then in another circle in the other direction. She pawed at the pillow until it turned over, and then she sniffed the couch, and then she walked along to the other end and jumped off.

Uh-oh, I thought. Trumpet was definitely no fat little Pekingese.

I followed her from room to room as she sniffed everything. I was worried she might pee on something, even though we let her out in the yard for a long time before she came in. But I knew that was something dogs did sometimes. And I definitely didn't want her to pee on my bed! Or my piano. Or on any of my stuff.

She could pee on Isaac's bed, though. That would show him for getting so excited about this dog. He wouldn't leave her alone. He kept yelling and startling her.

"Do a trick, Trumpet! Do a trick!" Isaac shouted. Trumpet gave him a funny, puzzled look. With the cute wrinkles between her eyes, it was almost like she was frowning at him.

"You have to teach her a trick first, Isaac," Dad said patiently.

"Can't she do anything cool?" Isaac demanded. "Shake hands! Play dead!" he bellowed at her.

Trumpet came over and sat on my foot. She leaned against my knee as if we were on the same side against Isaac. I kind of liked that.

"We should start with sit," Dad said. "Let's get some cheese."

All three of us followed him into the kitchen. Trumpet wagged her tail when Dad took a piece of American cheese out of the refrigerator. He broke it into small pieces. She watched him intently.

"All right, Trumpet," he said. "Sit."

Trumpet wagged her tail and stared at him.

"Sit," Dad said, holding the cheese in one hand and pushing her rump down with the other hand. He had to push pretty firmly, but finally she sat down. Then he gave her the cheese.

"Awesome!" Isaac yelped. "Do it again!"

"OK," Dad said, but now Trumpet was sitting. We had to pick her up and make her stand again, and then Dad shoved her butt back down, going, "Sit! Sit!" So I think she was a little confused. I would be, if I were her.

"Well, this is thrilling," I said after a few rounds of sit-and-cheese. "Can I go practice?"

"Of course," Mom said from the doorway. Mom loves that I like practicing so much. She wants me to be a famous musician as much as I do. She says she listened to Mozart and Chopin and Beethoven and Stravinsky the whole time she was pregnant with me. She wouldn't let Dad play any of his "noisy" albums around her, in case it ruined my musical taste.

"Don't you want to play with Trumpet a bit more?" Dad asked.

"That's OK," I said, standing up.

"Yes, she shouldn't get too attached either," my mom said meaningfully. I knew that tone of voice. It meant Mom and Dad were going to have a long, boring conversation where they each said, "Well, *I* feel —" a lot. That's how they make all their decisions, but it takes hours. So I scooted out of there as quickly as I could. If Isaac got stuck in the middle, too bad for him.

Our music room is what my dad calls our "sun-room," because it has all these windows and it's usually filled with sunshine. Not that day, though. That day it was gloomy and wet outside. I like practicing when it's raining because it fits the slow, sad songs that I like to sing best.

One wall is a huge bookshelf with all my music books and CDs and a stereo with speakers and a record player so we can play my mom's really really *really* old albums. There are comfortable armchairs around the room so that my family can sit in here and listen to me play, although Isaac always pitches a fit when we do this.

The piano takes up half the room, all glowing black and shiny. I sat down on the bench and ran my fingers up and down the scales. This summer I spent one month at music camp, like I have for the last two summers. I like it there because that's the one place where it's not weird that I know every single Stephen Sondheim musical by heart. My best friend from music camp, Caroline, has this whole plan for us to move to New York and be Broadway stars together one day.

After I got home from camp, I went to my piano teacher twice a week and my voice teacher every Wednesday for two hours. I can't go that often during the school year because I have too much homework, so the summers are always very busy with music.

Mom also signed me up for a ballet class on Fridays during August. She said it would make me more graceful. She said I would learn to express my music through my movements as well.

Yeah. That didn't happen at all. I felt like a caterpillar in my leotard — a *short* caterpillar — and I think I moved about as gracefully as one, too. It was extra-awful because Tara Washington was also in the class. She's long and bendy and has perfect posture, and she giggled loudly every time I tried to do a plié. Tara and her best friend, Natasha, are not my favorite people, although they usually leave me alone if I stay out of their way. They're too busy thinking about boys, especially Parker Green, their latest obsession.

But now ballet was over and school was starting again and I had to focus on my music. Our school always has a Welcome Back Talent Show in the second week to get everyone excited for the new year. I don't think it gets anyone excited for school exactly, but it's fun to get up and perform.

I've done a song for the talent show every year

since first grade, but I've never won, no matter how much I practice or how much Mom tells me I'm wonderful.

Last year I played the piano and sang this pretty French song called "Barcarolle." It was really hard and I practiced it all summer and my teachers were all really impressed. But the talent-show judges gave first place to a trio of sixth-grade girls who dressed up in glittery dresses and lip-synched to a Hannah Montana song. My mom said that was "outrageous," but my dad said, "I thought they were kind of funny."

It didn't matter anyway. Now I was a sixth-grader, and those girls were gone, and this year was my last, best chance to win. I'd been working on a piece called "The Last Rose of Summer" that Charlotte Church sings, which is really pretty and sad. But I also liked "Alhambra," which is all in Spanish — I thought the judges might be impressed by that. My plan was to practice both of them until I had them absolutely perfect, and then decide which one to do.

I warmed up my voice a little and then started on the newest piece my piano teacher, Mrs. Mehta, had given me to practice. As my fingers hit the keys, I heard a jingle-jingling sound behind me. I glanced around and saw Trumpet come trotting into the room. She jumped up on the armchair in the corner. That's where Mom sits when she comes in to listen and give me advice.

"Are you a music critic, too, Trumpet?" I said, letting my hands play automatically. She cocked her head at me. It really looked like she was listening to the music.

"All right," I said, "what do you think of this?" I switched the pages on the piano over to "The Last Rose of Summer" and started to play. I took a deep breath and sang the first line of the song.

Trumpet cocked her head the other way. She lifted her nose a little and squeaked, "ooo ooo."

"Shush," I said and kept singing.

"AWROOOOOOOOOOOOOOOOOOOOOO!" Trumpet howled suddenly. She threw her head back so her ears flapped. Her mouth was wide open to the sky. And the noise she was making was the loudest, most awful, unmusical sound I had ever heard in my life.

I clapped my hands over my ears. "Trumpet!" I yelped.

"AWWUUGH AWWUGH," Trumpet kind of barked, kind of gurgled.

"I guess she hates it," Isaac said smugly from the doorway.

I stared at Trumpet. Trumpet stared back at me, panting, with a goofy dog grin on her face.

This was definitely going to be a problem.

CHAPTER 4

Mom came hurrying into the music room. "What was that horrible noise?" she said.

I pointed accusingly at the beagle. Trumpet lay down on the chair and covered her nose with her paws. Her enormous brown eyes seemed to get even bigger as she gazed up at us.

Mom crossed her arms. "Go ahead and play, Ella. I'll make sure she doesn't bother you."

I put my hands back on the keyboard. Trumpet sat up and leaned forward. I started to play.

"AUUUUUUUUUUUUUUUUUUUUUWHH, AUUUUUUUUUUUUUUUUUUGHUH," Trumpet howled. She threw her head back so violently that she nearly tipped over backward.

"No!" my mom said loudly, pointing at Trumpet. "No! Bad dog!"

"AUUUGH AUUUGH!" Trumpet barked back.

"All right, that's it," Mom said. She hooked her fingers in Trumpet's collar and dragged her off the chair and out of the room. "You will leave Ella alone to practice! Bad dog!" I could hear her scolding Trumpet as she dragged the dog away down the hall. "And that goes for you, too, Isaac!" Mom called over her shoulder. "Leave your sister alone!"

Isaac rolled his eyes. "Like I *want* to listen to her *stupid boring music* anyway," he said, but only loud enough so I could hear it and Mom couldn't. He stomped back to the kitchen.

Thank goodness for Mom. Otherwise I'd have no chance, between Isaac and Trumpet interrupting and bothering me. But now it was quiet again. I touched the keys lightly, calming myself down. Then I started to play from the beginning again. I sang as sweetly and sadly as I could.

"AWWWWWWWWUUUUUUUUUUUUU UUUUHHHHH AUUUUUUUUGH AUUU-UUUUUUUUUUUUWH!"

I couldn't believe it. Trumpet was howling so loud you could hear her all the way from the other side of the house. I mean, our house isn't very big, but Mom had dragged her upstairs. It wasn't as loud as when Trumpet was sitting right beside me, but it was still kind of like a fire engine and a foghorn were trying to kill each other in the next room.

I tried to play through it. I raised my voice and

sang as loud as I could. I banged on the piano keys and hit the pedal to make the sound reverberate. It's not the way you're supposed to play that song, but I figured I needed to do something to drown her out. Maybe if she saw that her noise was having no effect, she'd shut up.

No such luck. The louder I sang, the louder she howled. Plus it was a terrible way to rehearse. This wasn't how the song should sound at all!

Finally Dad came into the music room. He was rubbing his forehead like he had a headache. "Tell you what, superstar. Why don't you take a break for a little while?"

When I took my hands off the keys, Trumpet stopped howling. "But Dad, I have to practice! The talent show is less than two weeks away!"

"I agree with Ella," Mom said, joining us. She was frowning. "I tried to shut that dog in Ella's bedroom, but it doesn't seem to help. Maybe we should put her outside in the yard."

"But Glenda, it's pouring," Dad said. He pointed to the storm outside. "That would just be cruel." He looked at me pleadingly. "You wouldn't want to do that, right, Ella?"

I felt bad. I didn't want to upset Mom by stopping

my practice, but Dad was right — it would be mean to make Trumpet stay outside in this weather. I sighed. "I have some reading I could do instead," I said.

"That's my girl!" Dad said. He patted my head. "We'll try again later. Maybe Trumpet will be calmer by then."

She wasn't. As soon as I went back into the music room after dinner, Trumpet came galloping in and hurled herself onto the armchair. She sat down and looked at me like she couldn't wait for me to start playing.

I glared at her. "If you like it so much," I said, "why don't you shut up and let me play? You'd appreciate it a lot more if you could hear it! Believe me!"

"I think it's way better when Trumpet sings along," Isaac said snottily.

"Isaac, go away!" I snapped.

"AUWF AUWF," went Trumpet, like she agreed with me.

But she didn't agree about letting me practice. No matter what I played, as soon as I started to sing, she would throw back her head and join in. The weird thing was, she didn't do it when I played without singing. The piano by itself just made her cock her head, or lie down and listen politely. But there was something about singing that made her go bananas.

I hoped it wasn't just *my* singing. I know this will sound stupid, but I was kind of like, *Does this dog know something about my voice that all my teachers don't?*

"Maybe I'm not as good as I thought!"

"That's ridiculous," Dad said, tugging on one of my braids. "You're our little musical genius. Whose opinion matters more, mine or some dog's?" He sat down on the bench beside me and played a dramatic chord. Trumpet sat up. "Check this out," Dad said. He started to play "Great Balls of Fire." The minute he started to sing, Trumpet started to howl. He kept playing, and she kept howling all the way through.

"As if one tone-deaf howler wasn't bad enough," Mom joked when he finished. "But seriously, Ella, you know you're wonderful. Everyone agrees, even the premier music critic in the country." She was talking about herself. She jokes a lot about what an important critic she is, but it's true that lots of people who care about classical music read her online column like Mozart has come back from the dead to tell them what to think.

"Maybe she wouldn't howl at a *really* good singer, though," I said.

"Hey," Dad said, pretending to be offended.

"You *are* a really good singer, Ella," Mom said. "But here, let's test that theory." She put in a CD. Sure enough, as soon as Charlotte Church started singing, Trumpet began to howl.

That made me feel a little better. Only not really, because I realized that not only would it be impossible for me to practice, but now I couldn't even listen to my music. Trumpet would howl at everything.

I was beginning to think we couldn't have gotten a worse pet for this family. Surely Aunt Golda had noticed this problem of Trumpet's? What had she done about it? Why would she leave a disaster like this to me?

It got worse at bedtime. We didn't have a dog bed for her yet, and Trumpet didn't want to sleep in her traveling bag. Mom spread out a few towels on the floor of the kitchen and shut the door while Trumpet was sniffing them suspiciously.

Immediately Trumpet started howling. She howled and howled like someone was poking her with knitting needles or trying to steal her ears.

"Ignore her," Mom said. "She'll go to sleep eventually."

She didn't. Finally, after an hour, Dad went and

opened the door of the kitchen. He meant to yell at her, but as soon as the door moved, Trumpet shoved herself through the gap and galloped upstairs. She charged into my room, where I was sitting on my bed, reading one of our summer assignments for sixth-grade English. Trumpet practically threw herself under my bed.

Dad came running up behind her. "Where did she go?" he asked, panting. I pointed down at the floor under my bed.

Dad shook his head. "Maybe we should let her stay there," he said. "If it lets us all sleep. Would you mind?"

"I guess not," I said. "As long as she doesn't howl."

"I want her to sleep under *my* bed!" Isaac shouted, running into the hall in his bulldozer pajamas.

Dad steered him back to his room. "Maybe some other night, champ," he said as he tucked him back in.

I leaned over the edge of the bed, lifted up the blanket, and peered underneath. Trumpet was flopped out on the carpet under my bed. She looked asleep, but she opened her eyes when I peeked at her. Her tail swished back and forth.

"All right," I said. "But don't you dare make a

sound." I dropped the blanket. And I didn't hear a peep out of her for the rest of the night.

On Sunday it was still wet outside, but it wasn't pouring anymore. So we put Trumpet out in the yard while I practiced. At first I thought it was going to work. I got all the way to the third line of "Alhambra" before Trumpet's big ears heard me through the window. Then she came and sat down *right outside* the sunroom windows and howled and howled and howled. I could hear her perfectly clearly with all the windows closed. What was worse, so could all the neighbors. Finally Mr. Sorenstam next door called to beg for a little peace, and we had to bring Trumpet inside.

It was a mess. Trumpet howled when I tried to practice. She barked whenever we turned on the radio. Even the TV could make her go crazy if anyone tried to sing, like in show theme songs or commercials. We all took turns trying to make her shut up. Isaac yelled at her, but she just barked louder like she thought it was a volume competition. Mom tried to lock her into other rooms in the house, including the basement. That obviously didn't work because Trumpet hated it, and she made sure we all knew about it. Dad looked at Trumpet sternly and said, "Now, Trumpet, why don't you be a good dog for once?" (That's kind of how he disciplines us, too.)

Trumpet went: "AUUWWF!"

As for me, I tried to ignore her. But she followed me all over the house. I don't know what about me was so fascinating. I'm only interesting when I sing, and now I couldn't even do that, thanks to Trumpet. I tried to hide from her a couple of times, but she found me, wagging her tail every time.

By the end of Sunday, I was really tired. I needed a break. I needed to practice!

For the first time in my life, I couldn't wait for school to start.

CHAPTER 5

Dad knocked on my bedroom door to wake me up on Monday morning. I guess Trumpet thought we were being attacked, because she shot out from under the bed, barking like crazy. She threw herself at the door, "awuuu"-ing and howling. Dad opened it in a hurry.

"Shush, shush, shush!" he said, but it was too late. Trumpet had woken Mom. Normally Mom gets up after we leave for school. She rents an office downtown, where she goes to write during the day. The deal is that Dad takes us to school in the morning, and she picks us up again in the afternoon. That way she gets to sleep a little later.

But not this morning. And when Mom hasn't gotten enough sleep, she can be really cranky about it.

"Henry!" she hollered from her room.

"Sorry, honey!" Dad called back. "Ella, will you let Trumpet outside?"

I scrambled out of bed and went downstairs in my

pajamas. Trumpet thumped down the steps behind me, wagging her tail. I opened the door to the backyard, rubbing the sleep out of my eyes. Trumpet pushed past me and started trotting around the yard, nosing at the dandelions in the bright morning sunshine.

Suddenly I froze. There was someone in the yard behind mine. He was standing on his deck, like I was standing on mine. And now he was staring at me and my dog.

It was Nikos Stavros. He's in my grade at school. Even though his yard is right behind mine, we almost never see each other. I mean, there's not much reason to go into my yard. I'm usually inside, practicing my music. And he's usually inside, studying, as far as I know. He's one of the smartest guys in our class.

So what are the chances that he would be in his backyard right when I opened the door in my pajamas? I mean, right?

Not that I care. I'm not like Tara and Natasha, who obsess and giggle over boys all the time. I try not to pay attention to boys. They'll just distract me from my musical career.

But seriously! My pajamas have little cows playing musical instruments all over them!

Cows!

Plus my hair is always a gigantic curly mess first thing in the morning. I wanted to run inside, jump back into bed, and stay there for the rest of sixth grade. But he was already waving to me.

"Hey Ella!" he called. "Ready for the first day of school?"

"Yeah," I said, pointing at my pajamas. "Don't I look ready?"

He laughed. That made me feel a little better. But not a lot.

"Is that your dog?" he asked.

I'd nearly forgotten about Trumpet, what with all the emotionally scarring pajama trauma happening. "Oh. Yeah," I said. I tried to smooth down my hair, but I could feel it flipping up in ways that hair really shouldn't, at least not in front of boys. "I mean, sort of. For now."

"He's so handsome," Nikos said, leaning on the rail of his deck. Nikos can get away with saying words like "handsome" because he's cool as well as smart. I mean, if Parker Green likes him, you know he's cool.

And he's pretty good-looking. I wouldn't notice something like that, but Tara followed him around for a while last year, so he must be. He has dark hair and dark eyes and he looks kind of like that hot Greek guy in *The Sisterhood of the Traveling Pants.*

When Tara found out he lived behind me, she even tried to be friends with me so I'd invite her over. But there's not a lot to do at my house if you don't want to listen to Sarah Brightman CDs or play the piano. That's another reason I don't hang out with girls from school very much — I feel like we'd probably have nothing in common. Only my music-camp friends get me, and they all live in other states.

Anyway, I showed Tara my goldfish, and then she wanted to go "tan" on my deck, which was funny because her skin is already this perfect dark brown color. But she'd even brought a bikini to wear and everything. I told her I didn't "tan" and that too much sun was bad for your skin, and then she got kind of mad. So I let her go hang out on my deck by herself, but Nikos never came outside. I could have told her he hardly ever does.

She didn't come back after that.

"Actually, Trumpet's a she," I said to Nikos. "And we might not keep her. She's really loud."

"Oh, *that's* what I heard yesterday!" Nikos said, snapping his fingers. "I was thinking, gee, Ella's really out of practice."

"Ha-ha-ha," I said, but I couldn't help smiling at him. He has a cute smile. I mean, not that I noticed.

"Well, you should keep her anyway," he said. "She's cute."

Trumpet went up to the fence and wagged her tail at him like she understood.

"Yeah, we'll see," I said, smoothing my hair down again. "Come on, Trumpet!"

She came trotting back obediently.

Nikos waved again. "See you in school!" he called.

I took Trumpet back inside and went to look at myself in the mirror. Did I look as embarrassed — and as embarrassing — as I thought?

Oh, yes. My hair was in prime morning crazy mode. And I was blushing, so my face was all pink. I figured no one had ever had a more embarrassing dog.

That's what I thought until I got to school, anyway. I was in Mr. Peary's class, with Nikos and Parker and Tara and Natasha and Heidi and a bunch of other kids. Mr. Peary seemed interesting. He made us all move our desks into a U shape so we were all facing each other, which was cool because we'd never done something like that before. While we were moving our desks, Parker Green came in. He usually looks really calm, like nothing bothers him, but that day his hair was kind of windblown and he was breathing like he'd been running. He handed Mr. Peary a note and said that his dog had made him late.

I had no idea Parker had a dog. I was glad *my* dog hadn't made me late. Mom would have been really mad. She was already pretty grumpy about being woken up and about having to come home in the middle of the day to let Trumpet out.

My desk was on one end of the U, close to Mr. Peary's desk. Heidi Tyler pushed her desk in beside mine. She gave me a friendly smile. Heidi is nice to everyone. She's a little scary, though, because she's the tallest girl in the class — much taller than me — and she breaks things by accident all the time. I don't know what her science-fair project was last year, but whatever it was, it exploded during the fair, leaving mysterious smelly black-and-green goop all over Heidi and the judges. In case you're wondering, she didn't win. (Nikos did.) She's also the kind of girl whose soda can always sprays fizz all over everyone when she opens it. *Every single time.* I know she doesn't mean to be such a klutz, but it's still sort of dangerous to be around her.

Parker and Nikos were on the other side of the classroom, beside the windows. When I glanced over at them, Nikos actually smiled at me. I couldn't remember him doing that before. But then, I didn't usually look at him either.

"All right," Mr. Peary said. "Let's go around the room and introduce ourselves. Tell us your name and something interesting about yourself."

As usual, the only interesting thing I could think of about myself had to do with music, so I talked about the new songs I'd learned over the summer. Nobody looked very excited. But I was sure they would be once they heard me sing at the talent show.

Heidi went next. She stood up and said, "I'm Heidi, and this summer my family went to New Zealand, so I got to skydive — well, tandem skydive — and shear a sheep — well, hold a sheep while someone else sheared it — and climb a volcano and swim in the Pacific Ocean and see the place where they filmed a *Lord of the Rings* battle and it was totally awesome."

See, that was a *lot* more interesting than anything I could have said. I hoped I would have thrilling stories like that once I was world-famous and traveled everywhere to sing in concert halls and stuff. Great-Aunt Golda would have loved Heidi — Heidi was clearly "experiencing life to the utmost!" already.

But the story everyone got most excited about was Parker's, which was funny because it was the shortest.

He just stood up and said, "I'm Parker, and I have a new dog."

"What kind of dog?" Nikos asked.

"A golden retriever," said Parker. "His name is Merlin."

Heidi nearly fell out of her chair, she was so excited. I'm not exaggerating. Her chair tipped to the side and she had to grab her desk to stay upright. "Oh, wow!" she yelped. "That is so cool! I love dogs! I want one so badly!"

I realized I could have said I had a new dog, too. Then everyone might be asking me about Trumpet and what kind of dog she was. Maybe Nikos would say he'd seen her and Tara would be jealous. Maybe Heidi would be giving me all that hyperactive attention. But I didn't want that anyway. Did I?

That's when Natasha spotted a dog out on the playground. She pointed out the window and everyone got out of their seats to look. I wasn't sure if we'd get in trouble for doing that, so I stayed where I was. It turned out to be Parker's dog! He had to leave class and go get his dog from the playground in the middle of the school day. He looked really embarrassed about it, both when he left and when he came back, even though it just made everyone want to talk to him even more than they usually do. Parker can look cool no matter what happens to him. But if that had been me, I would have died of embarrassment. I would not have been able to come back to the classroom, I think. I would have been too sure that Tara and Natasha were making fun of me.

So I was lucky, I guess, that my dog wasn't *as* embarrassing as Parker's new dog.

But it was still a relief when lunchtime came, because it meant I could sneak off to the music room and practice. I ate my sandwich in the cafeteria as fast as I could. I used to sit with the other girls in my class at lunch, but then they would bother me and ask me a lot of questions if I tried to get up and go practice. It was like they thought it was *too* weird that I actually *wanted* to be playing piano. So it's easier to sit by myself. I can eat faster that way, anyhow.

I saw Heidi and Kristal and Rebekah sit with Parker and his friends. Tara and Natasha didn't like that too much. They probably wished they'd thought of it first. They kept whispering to each other and looking over at Parker's table. But Parker didn't notice. I thought that was kind of funny. Rebekah might have noticed — she's kind of quiet and sweet, and she's always trying to make people happy, so she pays attention to who is looking at her and what everyone is saying. Not Heidi, though. Heidi was too excited about Parker's dog to notice anything else. I wondered if she would think that Trumpet was "the most amazing fantastic beautiful thing she'd ever seen," too. Somehow I think Heidi would fall in love with any dog.

Then Heidi knocked over her tray and got green beans and milk all over the table and all over Danny and Kristal. See what I mean? It's not safe to be near her.

I hurried away to the music room soon after that. Miss Caruso, the music teacher, doesn't mind if I use it whenever I want to. Sometimes she's eating lunch in there and she listens to me play. But today the room was empty. I sat down at the piano and felt calm again, like I hadn't felt since Trumpet arrived. I warmed up my voice, played through both of my pieces, and felt a lot better.

The only problem was that I knew it couldn't last. After school I had my piano lesson. Then I'd go home, and Trumpet would be there. Usually I practiced until dinner, but if I tried to do that, the howling would drive me crazy.

What was I going to do?

CHAPTER 6

When the final bell rang, I got my stuff and walked slowly out to the parking lot. I spotted Isaac running around the playground with something pink and shiny in his hand. He was yelling, "Ha-ha! Can't catch me! Ha-ha!"

"Isaac Finegold!" a girl's voice screamed. *Uh-oh*. I ran over and saw Rosie Sanchez throwing a major temper tantrum. Her older brother is Danny, who's in my grade. Rosie is in fifth grade. I don't know why Isaac was bothering a fifth-grader. Especially Rosie. He really should know better than that.

"Give it back RIGHT NOW!" Rosie yelled, stamping her foot. "Isaac, you little brat!"

"She should talk," Danny joked. He was sitting on the wall, probably waiting for Parker. And he was staying well out of his sister's way.

Isaac didn't see me coming. He was racing around the slide, waving his prize in the air, and he ran right into me. I grabbed his grubby little hand and realized he was clutching a sparkly pink ribbon. No mystery where that had come from. Rosie wears pink pretty much every day, almost always with a matching ribbon in her hair.

"OW!" Isaac roared.

"What is the matter with you?" I said. "Why are you torturing Rosie?"

Rosie stormed up and yanked the ribbon out of his hand. "From now on, you leave me alone, you horrible little monster," she said fiercely.

"Say you're sorry," I said, shaking Isaac's arm.

"I was just *playing*," Isaac protested. "*Jeeeeeeeeeeeeeeeeeeeeeeeeeeez.*"

"I wouldn't accept his apology anyway," Rosie said, sticking her nose in the air. She stomped away again, smoothing the pink ribbon between her fingers. Danny gave me a shrug from the top of the wall.

Beep beep. Mom's car pulled up to the curb. She peered out the window at us.

"You're in trouble now!" Isaac shouted. He jerked himself free and ran over to the car. By the time I caught up, he was in the front seat, spinning a tale of woe about how mean I was and how I'd hurt his arm and *whine whine blah blah blah.*

"Ella, that wasn't very nice," Mom said with a little frown.

"Well, *he* wasn't being very nice!" I said. "Did he tell you he stole Rosie's ribbon? I was just getting it back for her."

"I'm sure Rosie can take care of herself," Mom said, but she was clearly distracted. She kept leaning forward and looking at the other kids coming out of school. And the car wasn't moving, even though Isaac and I were all the way in.

"Mom? Why aren't we going?" I asked. "I'm going to be late for my piano lesson."

"I told Mrs. Mehta we could give Pradesh and Kamala a ride home, since I'm driving you over there anyway," Mom said.

"Oh, *Mooooooooooooooom*," Isaac and I both cried at the same time. For once, we agreed about something — that this was an enormously embarrassing thing for Mom to do. Pradesh Mehta is in my grade, although he's in Mr. Guare's class. And his little sister, Kamala, is in Isaac's grade. If anyone saw us giving them a ride home, they'd be all "Ooooooh, Ella likes Pradesh" and "Kamala has a boooooooyfriend" and we'd never hear the end of it.

Of course, by "anyone" I mean Avery Lafitte. Avery is the meanest, most awful person I've ever met. He's kind of big and red-faced with squinty little eyes and he's a jerk to everyone all the time. Last year after the talent show, I went back to my locker to get a book, and he was in the hall, kicking doors. I don't know why. He's just angry all the time. He saw me go up to my locker, and he was like, "Hey Ella, what was that song you played?"

So I said, "It's called 'Barcarolle.' It's French," because I'm polite like that.

And he said, "It should be called 'BORING-ROLLE'! Way to put the whole audience to sleep, Finegold! Couldn't you tell that everyone hated it? It was totally stupid!"

I slammed my locker door and said, "Shut up, Avery!" And then I ran away. I've never been so upset in my whole life. I had to go hide in the bathroom for a while so no one would see me crying. I think my mom thought I was upset because I didn't win. But really it was because of what he said. I couldn't stop thinking about it. I *still* think about it all the time. I mean, why would anyone do that? There's no reason to go around just being mean to random people. But what if he was right? Was I that terrible? How would I know? Mom and Dad said they loved it. But wouldn't they say that anyway? Sometimes when I'm trying to fall asleep, I remember what he said and how he looked all mad when he said it, and then I can't fall asleep for hours because I lie there worrying about it.

Anyway, he's a jerk, is my point. And he would definitely tease me for hanging out with Pradesh. Pradesh is OK, but he's not cool at all. He was our school spelling-bee champion last year (he beat all the sixth-graders, too) and he acts kind of nervous and jumpy all the time so it's hard to talk to him, plus he likes to use a lot of big words. It seems like he's always studying for spelling. Avery would probably say we're a perfect match, because Avery doesn't know anything about me at all.

"Pradesh!" my mom yelled, rolling down the car window. "Over here!"

I wanted to melt into the floor. But it would look even sillier to hide, so I just kind of slouched as low as I could while Pradesh and his sister climbed into the backseat with me. Kamala sat in the middle. She gave me a big smile. Pradesh looked as embarrassed as I was. He pulled his hair over his face like he was trying to hide behind it, but it isn't long enough for that.

"Hi Ella!" Kamala said. Her black pigtails swung around as she grinned at all of us. "Hi Isaac! Hi Mrs. Finegold!"

"Hey," I mumbled. Isaac dramatically buried his head in his hands and didn't answer. Kamala didn't seem bothered by this.

"Ella, have you decided which song to play at the talent show?" she asked, but she chattered on without waiting for me to answer. "Mom says I'm ready to do a piece if I want, but I'm so nervous! I hope they don't put me next to you on the program, because you're so good I'll just sound terrible!"

"Are you kidding?" I said. "You're a great piano player. You should definitely do it. It'll make me practice even harder knowing I'll have such tough competition."

Kamala grinned wider and wriggled her shoulders. "I told Pradesh he should get up and spell some really hard words. Wouldn't that be funny?" She wound one of her pigtails around her fingers and gave him a sly look.

"Yeah, ha-ha," Pradesh said, scowling.

Kamala chattered all the way to her mom's house. That was kind of a relief, because it meant I didn't have to make awkward small talk with Pradesh. He bolted from the car as soon as we pulled up. By the time Kamala and I got inside, he was already hiding up in his room. Which was so fine by me.

I like the Mehtas' house because Mrs. Mehta is an amazing cook, so the whole place always smells spicy and exciting. Sometimes after the lesson she gives me samosas or chutney or something to take home with me. She's also a lot nicer than my last piano teacher, Mr. Cricket. Mom worries that she's not challenging me enough, but I think she is.

We went through the pieces I'd been practicing at home. Now that I'd thought of him, I couldn't get Avery out of my head, so I made a few mistakes. The word "BORING!" kept flashing in my mind and my fingers would stumble on the keys.

Mrs. Mehta patted my hand. "All right, take a break. Is everything all right, Ella? You seem to be having trouble concentrating today."

I didn't want to tell her about Avery — I hadn't told anyone about that — so instead I found myself telling her all about Trumpet and how I was worried that I wouldn't get to practice anymore if the dog was always howling.

"Surely there's a solution," Mrs. Mehta said. "Lots of people with dogs can still practice. You just have to figure out how to stop her."

Which wasn't very helpful.

By the time Mom came to get me, I was feeling kind of unhappy and clumsy and untalented. I said good-bye to Mrs. Mehta and ran down to the car. To my surprise, Mom had brought Trumpet with her. The beagle threw herself against the passenger-side window when she saw me. I could hear her barking up a storm as I hurried across the lawn. Her tail was wagging like crazy and her paws scrabbled against the window like she thought she could dig her way out before I got there.

When I opened the car door, Trumpet practically flew into my arms. She knocked my piano books to the ground and clambered all the way up to my face, making those funny happy squeaking sounds. I felt her tongue slurp along my cheek. Even though it was totally ridiculous, I started laughing. I couldn't help it. No one had ever been this happy to see me before. I was sure I hadn't done anything to deserve it.

"Oh my word," Mom said, getting out of the car. She came around to help pick up my books. "This *dog*. I have never *met* such a lunatic animal. She's been searching for you all afternoon, ever since Isaac and I got home. She sat by the door for a while, and then she ran up to your room as if maybe you'd gotten past her. She checked under your bed and on top of your bed and in your closet, and then she ran all over the house, and then she went back and sat by the door again for a while, until she decided to do all that over again. Round and round and around, so I finally decided to let her come with me to pick you up. I hoped that would calm her down, but so much for that plan!"

Trumpet had her front paws up on my right

shoulder now and her face snuggled into my neck. My arms were wrapped around her, holding her up, even though she was a little too big for that to be comfortable.

"You were looking for me?" I asked Trumpet, amazed. Her tail swished back and forth like a metronome. "Why on earth do you like me so much?" When I talked to her, she licked my neck and made me giggle.

Mom put my books in the backseat while I scooted into the car, holding Trumpet on my lap. Her velvety ears brushed my cheek, and her fur was warm under my fingers. "Is it because you think we're fellow musicians?" I whispered to her as Mom went around the car. "Maybe we both think we're more talented than we actually are." Trumpet licked my nose.

"Don't think this makes up for interrupting my rehearsal," I warned her. I was still worried about when I would get to practice, if there was going to be a dog howling in the background all the time.

But I had to admit — Trumpet being so happy to see me cheered me up a lot. As we drove home, and she curled up closer to me, I realized that I felt much better.

Avery Lafitte might not like me, but Trumpet definitely did.

CHAPTER 7

It seemed like thinking about Avery made him appear, like an evil spirit conjured by my mind. I was just sitting by myself at lunch on Tuesday, minding my own business, when I saw him sit down at Parker's table. He wasn't there long before Heidi snapped at him and he stood up in a hurry. He looked all mad, the way he usually does. I focused on my peanut-butter sandwich.

Don't come over here, I prayed. *Don't notice me. Leave me alone.*

"Hey Finegold." His awful deep voice sneered at me. I didn't look up at him. "Whatcha doing? Dreaming about Mozart? Composing stupid symphonies in your head? Wishing you had friends?"

What would Parker do? Or Heidi? They'd ignore him, right?

Avery reached out with one big meaty hand and swiped my whole lunch onto the floor. Everything hit the ground except the sandwich I was holding in my hand: a bag of carrots, a yogurt, a bag of chips, and one of the brownies Dad had made last night. The carrots and chips spilled all over the tiles.

"Oops," Avery said meanly. "You made a mess, Finegold. I guess you should clean it up."

I stood up, pushed past him, and hurried out of the cafeteria. I was still holding the rest of my sandwich in my hand, but I wasn't hungry anymore. I threw it in a trash can on the way to the music room.

Sitting at the piano didn't make me feel as good as it usually did. I wished I had someone to talk to. I wanted to tell someone what Avery had done. Someone who would laugh and say he was a jerk and make me feel better.

Trumpet would make me feel better. That was a strange thought, considering we'd only had her for four days and she was such a pain in the neck. I pictured the way she looked at me and remembered the weight of her head resting on my lap while we watched TV. My breathing started to slow down. Soon I wasn't about to cry anymore.

I figured I should go back and clean up my spilled lunch. I felt bad about leaving it for the custodians. But I wanted to wait until Avery was gone, so I played a few things until the lunch hour was nearly over. Then I went back to the cafeteria and peeked in. Most of the younger kids had gone out to the playground, while some of the older ones were still sitting at their tables, talking. I didn't see Avery anywhere.

It wasn't until I nearly got back to my table that I realized someone was there, picking up carrots from the floor and throwing them at the nearest trash can. It was Pradesh. I think I would only have been more surprised if it had been Avery.

"Pradesh?" I said.

He jumped and kind of toppled over sideways, then scrambled to his feet, wiping potato-chip crumbs off his jeans.

"Hey," he said. "Um. Yeah. Just helping."

"Thanks," I said, and I meant it. "I didn't mean to leave such a mess." I crouched down and started putting crumbs into a paper napkin.

"Yeah, I saw Avery," Pradesh said awkwardly. He was really tall. He might even be taller than Heidi. I'd never noticed that before. "What he did, I mean. He's done that to me, too. He's a lummox."

"A what?" I said. See what I mean about the big words? I didn't know what this one meant, but I liked the sound of it.

"A stupid jerk," Pradesh said. Even though I was still upset, I laughed. It was funny to hear Pradesh *not* using fancy words.

"He's a big lummox," I agreed. I felt bad that I'd never noticed Avery being mean to Pradesh. I mean, I knew he was like that to everyone, but I thought most people didn't care as much as I did.

"OK. I should go — class," he said. He tugged on one of his backpack straps.

"Thanks again," I said. "Seriously." He shrugged and lobbed another carrot into the trash can with perfect aim.

"Nice. You should try out for the basketball team," I said.

"Nah. I have to study for the spelling bee," he said. His face lit up a little. He looked about as excited as Pradesh ever does. "I want to win the national bee in DC this year."

"Oh," I said. "OK. Good luck."

He lifted his shoulders again and kind of loped away. I glanced around, but nobody was looking our way. Luckily Tara and Natasha were gone. Like Avery, they can pick up on anything potentially embarrassing from, like, five hundred miles away.

I managed to finish cleaning up and got back to Mr. Peary's classroom before the bell rang. I tried to focus on the positive. At least Avery wasn't in my class. At least Trumpet would be excited to see me when I got home.

I doodled musical notes all over my notebook while Mr. Peary talked about what we were going to read that year. I tried to draw little trumpets, but all my artistic talent is musical, so they looked kind of demented. Heidi glanced over a couple of times like she was trying to figure out what I was doing, but she didn't say anything.

So when I walked into my house that afternoon, I was feeling kind of warm and fuzzy toward Trumpet and we did a lot of hugging and jumping up and down together. That lasted until I sat down at the piano. I *had* to practice. I hadn't been able to concentrate properly during lunch, and I had less than two weeks until the talent show. Plus if I go too long without playing, I get really restless and nervous.

Trumpet lay down on the armchair. She propped her head on her paws and gave me an innocent expression.

"No singing along," I warned her, trying to look stern. "Just listen. Be a good dog."

Trumpet tilted her head to the side and blinked.

I played a few pieces without singing. When I looked over, Trumpet's eyes were closed. Perfect. If she just kept sleeping, she'd be a great dog.

I put up the "Alhambra" music and started to play. Barely two notes were out of my mouth when . . .

"Auuuwwwwwh auuuuuuwwwwgh! AAAUUU-UWWWWH! AUUUUWWGUUUH!!"

"Trumpet! No!" I scolded. "Bad! Bad!"

"AUWF! AUWF!" she answered like she was agreeing with me . . . or maybe mocking me, it was hard to tell.

"Why are you so bad? Hush up and listen!" I said.

She lay down again, as if she had no idea what I was getting so agitated about.

I tried again. And again. And again. But every time, as soon as I opened my mouth, so did Trumpet. She howled gleefully through every song I tried to sing. My ears were ringing when I stopped. I couldn't even get Mom to help, because she was with Isaac at his soccer practice. I was the only one at home. Me and the noisiest dog on the planet.

"All right, come with me," I said, standing up. Trumpet jumped off the chair right away. She trotted behind me up the stairs. I led her into Mom and Dad's room and then over to their bathroom, which is as far away from the music room as you can get. Trumpet was instantly suspicious. She stopped next to Mom and Dad's bed and stared at me.

"Come on, Trumpet," I said, pointing into the bathroom. "In you go."

She sat down.

"In!" I said. "If you can't be quiet, this is what happens."

Trumpet lay down, and then started slowly crawling under the bed, like she hoped maybe I wouldn't notice if she just vanished.

I ran over and grabbed her around her middle before she got all the way under. I dragged her out and picked her up. She flailed wildly in my arms, trying to get free. I hurried over to the bathroom and dropped her on the mat on the floor.

"Now stay!" I said. "And quiet! Shush! Stay here and sleep or something like a normal dog!"

Trumpet made a dash for the door, but I jumped in her way. She stuck her nose between me and the wall, trying to squeeze by. I pushed her back onto the mat, leaped into the bedroom, and shut the door fast.

"OOOOOOOOOOOOOOOOUUUUUUUUU-UUUUUWWWWWWWWWWWWW," Trumpet protested at the top of her lungs. *I'm so looooonely! I'm so abaaaaaandoned! Why would you doooooooooo this to me?*

I hurried out of the bedroom and shut that door, too. If I shut the door to the living room and the door to the music room, that would make four doors between me and Trumpet, plus an entire floor. Surely then I could get some quiet.

But that didn't work at all. Trumpet didn't even wait for me to sing. She just howled and howled. She did *not* like being shut up in my parents' bathroom. She was so loud, I was pretty sure all the neighbors could hear her for blocks and blocks. I wondered if Nikos was home next door and what he thought about all the noise. It sounded like I was torturing her. Actually, it sounded like I was torturing a whole squadron of beagles and maybe a couple of dying hippos as well. Seriously, it was really loud.

Finally I stomped back upstairs and let her out. She was *so* excited to see me. You could tell she'd forgotten that I was the one who'd put her in there in the first place. She leaped and jumped and spun and danced all around me, squeak-barking happily.

"Well, I'm not pleased to see *you*," I said to her, but that didn't make any difference.

I was too frustrated to even try playing anymore, so I went to my room and lay down on my bed, pulling my musical-note blanket around me. Bird blooped bubbles at me from my desk. My calendar of famous music venues seemed to be staring at me accusingly like, *You'll never get to the Belfast Grand Opera House that way, missy.*

Trumpet galloped in and jumped up beside me. She flopped right down and rested her head on my stomach. She heaved a big sigh and gave me a look with her big brown eyes like she was saying *We've both had a tough afternoon, huh? Isn't it nice that now we can relax and recover together?*

"You know, *you're* the one stressing me out," I said. "Why can't you be more like Bird? Look at him swimming around peacefully. Look at how nice and quiet he is." She wagged her tail. She didn't seem to feel very guilty. Part of me wanted to shove her off the bed, but I didn't have the energy. And it was kind of nice having something warm snuggled up next to me.

So that's where Mom found us when she got home. She was about as pleased as Trumpet was about being shut in the bathroom. She couldn't believe I hadn't practiced at all, although I tried to tell her that at least I'd played the piano for a while. And then she found out that Trumpet had shredded all the toilet paper while she was in Mom's bathroom. I didn't know dogs could howl and shred toilet paper at the same time, but I guess Trumpet is multitalented.

"That's it," Mom said, putting her hands on her hips. "We can't have our whole lives disrupted like this. After the will reading on Thursday, we're finding Trumpet a new home."

CHAPTER 8

Isaac whined and screamed and threw a temper tantrum when he heard that Mom wanted to get rid of Trumpet. You would think the dog had saved him from a sinking ship the way he carried on and on. He could have competed with Trumpet for loudest nuisance on the block.

Dad didn't like the idea either. He thought we should give Trumpet more of a chance to be a good dog. Mom said she didn't want us getting attached and she didn't think there was anything we could do to fix Trumpet.

I didn't know what to think. My music is really important to me, and Trumpet could be a real pain in the neck. But when she wasn't interrupting my practice, I kind of liked her. Maybe I kind of liked her a lot. Maybe I was already "attached." She jumped up and sat on my lap while Mom and Dad and Isaac were arguing about her. She leaned against me, and when I put my arms around her, she licked the inside of my elbow. I mean, how funny is that?

So I didn't say anything. I figured I would wait to see what happened next. Maybe there was a way to make Trumpet a better dog. But I had no idea where to start.

The next day was Wednesday, and it turned out to be the craziest school day of all time. We were all in the cafeteria at lunch, eating our sandwiches and meat loaf like normal, when all of a sudden I heard some of the kids shouting, "Dog! Dog!" And then Troy Morris hollered, "FOOD FIGHT!" at the top of his lungs, and everything just went haywire.

This has happened before at our school. Food fights, I mean. But we've never had a food fight with a big golden retriever running through the middle of it! Yup, it was Parker Green's dog, back again. Parker looked fit to explode. You could tell he had no idea how his dog had gotten there. But Merlin went running up to him and then suddenly there was food flying all over the place.

Well, I know a messy situation when I see one, so I hightailed it out of there. I managed to run to the exit before anything hit me — which was lucky, because I'm sure Avery would have plastered me with something if he'd had half a chance. I hurried down the empty hall and into the music room. It would be much safer there. You couldn't even bring food into the music room, let alone throw it around.

I went over to the piano and sat down. There was some unfamiliar music sitting on the piano bench, so I started flipping through it. I figured Miss Caruso was going to teach us something new.

Suddenly the door to the music room flew open. Parker Green and his dog burst in. Parker didn't even see me. He practically dove headfirst behind the piano, dragging his dog behind him. There was a kind of crashing *thump* and then a long silence. All I could hear was Parker and the dog panting.

I wondered what I should do. Did he know I was here? It didn't seem like it. Should I pretend I wasn't here? Surely he'd notice me eventually. This was weird. When had I ever been alone in a room with Parker Green? I didn't know what the proper etiquette was for a situation like this. Talk to him? Hide? Pretend I was in a coma? I leaned out a little to see if I could see them behind the piano.

Parker jumped a mile when he spotted me. He kind of grabbed his chest like I'd given him a heart attack.

"Hi," he said.

"Hey Parker," I said, trying to act like I have

casual conversations with guys like Parker Green every day. "So, I'm guessing you're not here to practice for the talent show."

He smiled. "Just catching our breath," he said. His dog licked his face, and Parker rubbed the dog's head.

"That's your new dog?" I asked.

"Yeah," Parker said. "Merlin. The biggest troublemaker in dog history." Merlin wagged his tail like he was really proud of that title.

"You should meet mine," I said, and then I wondered if he would think I was, like, asking him out or something. I just meant that Trumpet was trouble, too, but what if Parker took it the wrong way?

"You have a dog?" Parker said. "But I thought you didn't like dogs."

Whew. He didn't notice.

"I don't really," I said. "Especially this one. We inherited her a few days ago. She's a royal pain." Except . . . did I really mean that? I watched Parker put his arm around Merlin. They looked totally perfect together. I couldn't believe Parker had never had a dog before. He seemed like the type of guy that any dog would love. And he's kind of outdoorsy and outgoing. A great dog owner. Not like me. What kind of dog would want to spend five hours a day lying around while I played piano? Lying around quietly, I mean. No, Trumpet and I were definitely a mismatch. But looking at Parker and Merlin, I kind of wished that people could see me and Trumpet that same way.

"They're worth it, though," Parker said. "I think. I hope. Eventually." His dog grinned at me.

"I doubt it," I said. "I mean, mine, anyway. This is the only place I can get any peace and quiet from her."

"Sorry to bother you," Parker said, and I felt bad. I didn't mean that *he* was interrupting me. Parker Green could interrupt me *anytime*.

"That's OK," I said. He kind of looked like he wanted to get out of there, so I asked if he wanted me to check whether the hall was empty.

"Would you?" he said. "Really?"

"Sure," I said, getting up from the piano bench. "Stay there."

When I opened the door, I saw our vice principal, Mr. Taney. He was sneaking down the hall, peering through the window of each classroom. Pretty soon he would be at the music room. And Merlin's long golden tail was clearly sticking out from behind the piano.

"Hi Mr. Taney," I said really loud, so Parker could hear me, too. "Why are you tiptoeing down the hall?"

"Hssssst," Mr. Taney said, flapping his hands at me. He frowned so his bushy white eyebrows kind of squished together. "Have you seen a dog come this way, Miss Finegold?" he demanded.

"A dog?" I said, trying to make my eyes big and innocent like Trumpet's. "Do you mean a hot dog? I think it was meat loaf day today, sir, not hot dogs."

"No, no!" Mr. Taney snapped. "An actual dog! Fur! Paws! Drool! Sanitation hazard!"

"A *real* dog!" I said, opening my eyes even wider. "What kind of dog?"

"Any kind of dog!" Mr. Taney shouted, exasperated. He grabbed his hair, which made it stick out like dandelion fluff. "If you've seen *any dog* running down this hallway, I want to know about it!"

"Gee, I'm sorry, Mr. Taney," I said. "I haven't seen any dogs running down this hallway. I didn't mean to make you *shout* at me." I tried to look like I was about to cry. Mr. Taney doesn't care if he makes kids cry, but he doesn't usually stick around to watch it happen.

"They must have gone the other way," he muttered. "I'll go around and cut them off!" He turned and hurried down the hallway.

I waited until he turned the corner, and then I

went back into the music room to tell Parker the coast was clear.

"That was awesome! You saved our butts," Parker said. "You should be an actress! You're totally hilarious."

I wondered if he could tell that my face was turning pink. No one had ever called me hilarious before. Sometimes I play funny songs to make my little cousins laugh, but they're three and five, so they pretty much laugh at everything. And this was Parker Green! Parker Green thought I was funny! When I wasn't even trying to be!

I didn't know what to say. *Yeah, I am hilarious? You're right, I did just save your butt?* Nothing I could think of sounded cool enough. Finally I mumbled something like, "Oh, I just like to sing."

"Well, thanks," Parker said. "See you later."

And just like that, he was gone.

It was weird. I'd only had Trumpet for five days, but it felt like things were really different. I wasn't practicing for three or four hours a day like I usually do. Boys like Nikos and Parker were having normal conversations with me. Someone was really excited to see me when I got home from school. The inside of my elbow had been licked.

And that was only the beginning of how Trumpet would change everything.

That afternoon, our new principal, Mrs. Hansberry, made us all help to clean up the cafeteria. I could have complained that I didn't throw any food. I could have said I was in the music room the whole time. Miss Caruso would have backed me up. They might have let me go practice for that hour instead of cleaning.

But I knew that a lot of other kids hadn't thrown any food either, and they still had to help. So I figured I should just join in. It couldn't be any worse than gym class, which I hate more than anything in the world.

Mr. Peary split us into groups. I got sent to wipe down some of the bright orange chairs with Heidi and Nikos. One of the janitors gave us a couple of sponges, a roll of paper towels, and a bucket of water. Of course, Heidi knocked the bucket over before we even got to the first table. Luckily I managed to jump out of the way, but Nikos's shoes got pretty wet. Heidi said she was sorry a million times, and Mr. Peary said something nice about how they needed to mop the floor anyway.

That made me kind of nervous about working next to her. I always think she's going to knock *me* over. I mean, she's really tall, and I'm pretty short. She might drop a sponge on my head without noticing I was there.

I think Nikos might have been thinking the same thing, because he gave her the paper towels. "Maybe Ella and I can clean the chairs, and you can dry them off," he said to her.

"OK!" Heidi said with a smile. I don't know if she could tell that he was trying to keep her out of trouble, but she didn't seem to mind.

I took one of the sponges, got it wet, and squeezed it over the new bucket of water. Nikos lined up the chairs in a row so we could do them all quickly. I told you he's pretty smart. He thinks about everything like it's a math problem — and he's really good at math.

"Hey Ella," Nikos said, "how's your dog? I heard her howling yesterday."

There was an enormous crash behind us. I turned around and saw that Heidi had knocked over about six chairs trying to get to me.

"You have a dog?" she said breathlessly. "What kind of dog? Since when? What's her name? Can I meet her?"

I swear she was nearly as excited as Trumpet. If Heidi had a tail, it would be wagging all the time.

And it would go into hyperdrive whenever someone mentioned dogs.

"Her name's Trumpet," I said.

"She's really cute," Nikos said. He smiled, and it gave me a weird happy tingly feeling to think that Nikos was the only person here who'd met my dog. (Well, and Isaac, who was picking meat loaf bits off the windows at the other end of the room. But annoying little brothers definitely do not count.) It was like we were friends or something.

"She's a beagle. She howls a lot," I said to Heidi.

"Oh my gosh, beagles are *so adorable*," Heidi said. She was squeezing the paper towels so hard she left finger dents in them. "I saw the one that won the dog show and I thought it was the cutest thing I'd ever seen and I can't believe you didn't tell me and Ella please please please say I can come over and meet your dog. Please?"

"Um, sure," I said. Heidi? At my house? I was pretty sure she had never been to my house before, even though we've been at the same school for like six years. Would my stuff be safe? What if she accidentally set my piano on fire? But she looked really thrilled. And I kind of liked the idea of showing off Trumpet. "Yeah, OK, you can come meet her. She's really loud, though. I'm just warning you."

"That's OK!" Heidi said. "How about today? After school? My mom won't mind. I was going to go to the baseball game but I can totally skip it, because, I mean, to meet your dog, that would be so much more fun!"

"I can't today," I said. "I have a singing lesson."

"OK, tomorrow's fine with me, too," Heidi said. "This is so amazing! I can't believe you have a dog! I'm so jealous!"

I'm afraid we didn't get a lot of cleaning done. Heidi kept asking me questions about Trumpet while I wiped down the chairs. She accidentally threw the paper-towel roll across the room once when she got really hyper and flung her hands in the air. It whacked Yumi Matsumoto in the head. Yumi didn't look pleased, but I think she was lucky it was just paper towels and not a sponge or green beans or a chair or something. With Heidi, you never know.

When the bell rang for the end of school, Heidi said, "Have a great singing lesson, Ella! I can't wait until tomorrow! I'm so excited!" She ran off to the baseball field before I could say anything, like maybe, *Are you sure you want to come over?* or, *Did I actually say yes to tomorrow?*

Nikos grinned at me. He took the sponge from my hand and dropped both of them in the bucket of water. "Heidi will love Trumpet," he said. "Maybe I'll see you guys out in your yard."

"Sure," I said. My head was spinning a little bit. I couldn't believe Heidi Tyler was coming to my house tomorrow. To meet my dog! I felt like a whole other person — someone who played outside with friends and a dog instead of practicing her music all the time. Maybe that's why I was brave enough to say to Nikos, "You can come over, too, if you want."

He gave me his cute smile again and said, "Yeah, OK, maybe I will."

I wondered what Tara would think of that!

CHAPTER 9

On Thursday morning, I told Trumpet she was getting a visitor. Trumpet wagged her tail and barked. She looked pretty happy. Then again, she looks like that when I say, "Time to do my homework" or "You are a very bad dog," too. I wish I always seemed happy. Like Parker and Heidi, who never get upset even when Avery teases them. I bet he'd leave me alone if he couldn't get a reaction out of me. But that's a lot easier to say than it is to do.

"How would you deal with a bully, Trumpet?" I asked her. I was still in bed. Trumpet's back legs were on the floor, but she had her front paws propped up on the mattress beside me and her long silky ears draped across the pillow. She blinked at me, and then pulled herself forward with her paws and licked my nose.

"Trumpet, yuck!" I said, rubbing my face. She wagged her tail. "Well, I don't think that would work with Avery," I told her. I couldn't even imagine walking up to Avery and licking his nose. The idea made me laugh, which was the first time thinking about Avery had ever made me laugh.

I made sure I was dressed and my wild hair was brushed and clipped back before I let Trumpet out into the backyard, but Nikos wasn't out there. While I ate my cereal, I told Dad that Heidi was going to come over after school.

To my surprise, this made him react as if I just told him I'd won a Tony Award.

"Really?" he said with a huge smile. "You have a friend coming over? Have we met Heidi before?"

"Maybe," I said with a shrug. "I went to her place for a party once. She's at all the talent shows and everything. She's the tallest girl in our class." I didn't tell him about her clumsiness. I didn't want him to worry about the safety of our furniture.

"Well, that is terrific!" he said. "That is great! I wish I could be here to meet her. Does she want to stay for dinner?"

"Let's not get carried away, Dad," I said. "She's only coming to meet Trumpet." And then she'd probably get bored and leave.

"Aww," Dad said, scratching Trumpet behind her ears. "Good dog, helping Ella make friends."

"I have friends!" I said. "I'm just busy most of the time, that's all. I'm concentrating on my music, Dad. These are important formative years for my career." That's something Mom says all the time.

"Well, remember to have fun, too," Dad said. "And if she does want to stay for dinner, we're having spaghetti and meatballs."

To tell you the truth, I was half-sure that Heidi would have forgotten about Trumpet by the time I got to school. She's always going so fast, I figure she must forget things all the time. But when I sat down next to her in class that morning, she was practically vibrating and humming like a harp string.

"Oh my gosh, I'm so excited," she said. Her red-blond hair was pulled back in a messy ponytail, like she couldn't find her brush that morning. "None of my other friends have dogs." She said "other friends" like I was one of her friends, without even thinking about it. "I mean, it's bad enough that Mom won't let me have one, but you'd think I'd know someone whose dog I could visit, wouldn't you? I can't believe Rory doesn't have one! She totally should. Or Kristal! You know?" Heidi lowered her voice, glancing around to make sure Tara and Natasha were talking to each other. "Tara let me play with her dog a couple of times, but she got bored of that and I didn't want to paint my nails or look at cute boys' MySpace pages. Plus, her dog is seriously crazy."

Uh-oh. "Mine's pretty crazy, too," I said warily.

"She can't be as bad as Bananas!" Heidi said. She leaned her chair back and called to Tara. "Hey Tara, isn't your dog totally insane?"

"Completely," Tara agreed, shaking her head so the beads on her braids clacked together. "This morning he got himself stuck between my bed and the wall. I mean, I have no idea how he did that! He was like howling and scrabbling and freaking out and my dad was like, 'Can't you control that dog?' and I was like, *'Hello,* it's not *my* fault he needs psychological help or whatever.'"

"Class," Mr. Peary said, tapping a ruler against his desk. "Time to settle down." The bell rang, and he picked up a pile of books on his desk. He went to the other side of the room, starting with Maggie, and gave one to each of us.

He had just gotten to Nikos when I looked down at my desk and saw a piece of paper that hadn't been there before. It took me a minute before I realized it was a note from Heidi. No one had ever passed me a note in class before. I felt kind of daring and wicked reading it, although it wasn't as if Mr. Peary was teaching us anything particularly important right then.

It said:

Anyway, thanks for having me over. I can't wait to meet your dog! It's so funny you have a beagle. I think I would have pictured you with a miniature schnauzer. Or a long-haired dachshund. Or a Yorkshire terrier. Something that looks small and quiet but has a big personality inside. Does that sound weird? Don't think it's weird. I think about dogs a lot. OK, THAT sounds weird, doesn't it? OK, I'll shut up now. I can't wait for school to be over! I wish it was 3:00 now!

I had no idea how to respond to that. Should I write back? What would I say? *What's a schnauzer? Yes, you are weird?* Luckily Mr. Peary got to us before I had a chance to do anything. He gave us each a copy of the book he was handing out. *Old Yeller.* It had a picture of a yellow dog on the front. Heidi's hand shot into the air.

"Yes, Heidi?" Mr. Peary said.

"I've already read this," Heidi said. "And I can't read it again. It's too sad."

"Don't give it away!" Danny yelled, clamping his hands over his ears.

"Oh, come on, Danny," said Virginia Marvell. She held up her copy of the book in a way that showed off her perfectly manicured fingernails. "You know if it's something we have to read, it's going to be sad. Especially if it's about a dog. We *always* have to read dog books, and they're always sad. That's why horse books are better."

"Not always," Heidi said quickly. "There are some really good books about dogs that aren't sad."

Mr. Peary rubbed his face like he was trying not to smile. "What would you suggest we read instead, Heidi?"

"Oh, um . . . *The Incredible Journey* is really good," Heidi said. "Or *White Fang*! I really liked that."

"Hey Mr. Peary, shouldn't you ask all of us what we think we should read?" Danny asked.

"Sure, Danny," Mr. Peary said. "Why, you have something in mind?"

"Um," Danny said. "OK, no. Not yet. But I'll think of something!"

Nikos raised his hand. "I think we should read *The Westing Game*," he said.

"Oh, I know, *20,000 Leagues Under the Sea*," said Jonas Mosley. He wants to be a marine biologist. His notebooks are all covered in drawings of fish and whales and octopi. We took a field trip to the aquarium last year and he got lost and nearly missed the bus home. I think he wouldn't have minded if we'd left him locked inside the aquarium all night.

"*The Black Stallion,*" said Virginia decisively.

"*I* think we should read *The Princess Diaries,*" Natasha said.

"*A Little Princess!*" Danny blurted. Parker and Eric and most of the other boys in the class started cracking up. "What?" Danny said. "Shut up! It's my sister's favorite book." He shoved Parker's shoulder. "Shut up, I couldn't think of anything else."

"All right, simmer down," Mr. Peary said. "I am curious to hear your ideas. So for the next fifteen minutes, write down a list of at least three books you think we could read in class and a reason why. They can be books you've read or ones you want to read. *Quietly,* now, boys," he said sternly as Danny gave Parker another shove. "I can't promise anything, but I'll think about whatever you suggest."

I turned to a blank page in my notebook and doodled a couple of musical notes in the margins. I tried to remember the last book I had read outside of school. There's this whole series of "shoes" books about talented orphans that I really like — *Ballet Shoes, Dancing Shoes, Theater Shoes* — but I wasn't sure if anyone else would have heard of them.

Another note slid slowly onto my desk. Heidi kept her eyes on Mr. Peary as she did it, making sure he wasn't watching us.

You should write down Shiloh*! said the note. It's about a beagle! It's awesome! P.S. Is this the longest day ever or what?*

We were barely half an hour into the school day. I wondered if Heidi had some kind of disorder that made a person hyper and clumsy and obsessed with dogs. But it was very cool of her to give me a book suggestion. I wrote down *Shiloh* at the top of my list. Heidi saw me do that and smiled.

She passed me two more notes before lunch. One said: *Check it out, Parker is so totally not paying attention again.* I glanced over at him. Heidi was right. He looked like he was drawing something in his notebook that probably had nothing to do with fractions. So I wrote *Yeah, totally* on the bottom of the note. I didn't know what else to say, but that seemed to be enough for her.

The next note said: *Almost lunchtime! Hooray!* Seriously, that was it. Heidi was too funny. I had seen other girls pass each other notes before, but I always thought they held big secrets or plans or something. Now I was starting to suspect that Tara and Natasha's notes to each other were probably as silly as their conversations.

Finally the end of the day came. Heidi leaped to her feet as soon as the bell rang, but she must have forgotten to zip up her backpack. Everything inside flew out and spilled all over the floor. Pencils and erasers and crumpled up papers and a yo-yo and a lip-gloss tube and about a zillion other things scattered everywhere.

"Oh, no!" Heidi cried. "I'm SUCH A MORON!" She ducked under her desk and started grabbing everything. I got down on the floor to help her.

"Thanks, Ella," Heidi said. "I can't believe I did that! Oh, hey, here's my brush. I was wondering where that was."

We were the last ones out of the classroom. Nikos waved to us as he left. Not that I cared, but it was the first time that had happened. Also the first time I found myself on the floor of a classroom picking up Skittles. We didn't try to save those.

"My mom doesn't let me have candy in the house," Heidi explained, "because this one time I left a Jolly Rancher on the carpet and it kind of melted and left, like, a bright green apple–smelling spot. Oh my gosh,

I got in so much trouble. We had to replace the whole carpet! So now I can only have candy at school, which is why there's so much of it in here." There really was a surprising amount of candy in her backpack. And even more in her locker, where we stopped on the way out. I couldn't believe how messy her locker was after only four days of school. It looked like a tornado had gone through it.

Outside, my mom was waiting in the car. Isaac had gotten there first and claimed the front seat again. Heidi and I got in the back. Mom turned herself all the way around to smile at Heidi.

"Hello Heidi, it's very nice to meet you," Mom said.

"*Mom*, you've met Heidi before," I said. "I mean, we've known each other, like, forever."

"What do you play?" Mom asked her.

"Play?" Heidi said, confused. "Oh — well, soccer. Although I'm not very good at it. Sometimes I kick the ball into the wrong goal. I just get excited and forget which way I'm supposed to go." She blushed and smiled and shrugged all at the same time.

Now it was Mom's turn to be confused. Even Isaac rolled his eyes.

"She meant what musical instrument," I said to Heidi. In Mom's world, everyone's life revolves around music. "Don't worry about it. Mom, not everyone is obsessed with music like we are."

"Oh," Mom said, but she still looked like she couldn't process that idea.

"I tried to learn the guitar once," Heidi offered. "But I broke a string and then my mom said I was being too loud anyway. Oooh, I'd love to play the drums, though! Wouldn't that be fun, Ella?"

Mom winced a little, but Heidi didn't notice. She kept talking as we pulled out of the parking lot. "I think it's so cool that your whole family is into the music thing. The only thing me and my mom and my dad definitely like to do together is travel, but we all have different ideas about where to go, so it takes ages and ages to decide."

"*I* don't like music," Isaac interrupted. "*I* think what Ella plays is *stupid*."

"Isaac!" my mom said. "Apologize to your sister!"

"Ella," Isaac said, "I'm sorry your music is stupid."

"*ISAAC!*" Mom said. Heidi laughed.

"Ignore him," I said to her. "He has no soul. There's peanut butter where his heart should be."

"Is Trumpet musical, too?" Heidi asked.

"Oh, you have no idea," I said.

Trumpet had her nose to the glass windows beside our front door when we pulled into the driveway. She stood up on her hind legs like she was trying to see us better. Heidi actually squealed when she spotted her.

"Oh my gosh!" she said, clutching my arm. "She's amazing! Look at those ears! Look at that tail! I love her already!"

We could hear Trumpet barking as we came up to the door. She jumped on me as soon as we got inside, trying to climb up and lick my face and run in circles all at once.

"Ohhh!" Heidi said, pressing her hands together. "Look how much she loves you!" She got down on her knees and Trumpet immediately jumped into her lap. Heidi scratched Trumpet's ears and rumpled her fur and rubbed her belly and Trumpet rolled around panting and loving it.

"All right, I have to go meet your father at the will reading," Mom said. "I'm dropping Isaac at Finn's house on the way. Will you two be all right for a couple of hours?"

"Sure," Heidi said. I nodded.

"Call me if you need anything, eat whatever you want, stay for dinner if you like," Mom said in a hurry and then she disappeared out the door, leaving me alone with accident-prone Heidi Tyler and my crazy, noisy beagle.

CHAPTER 10

I didn't even have a moment to feel awkward because right away Heidi said, "Let's take her outside! Can we?"

"Yeah, OK," I said. Trumpet trotted ahead of us to the back door and then hurled herself down the steps from the deck to the yard.

"Do you have a tennis ball?" Heidi asked. "Do you think she would chase it?"

"I don't know. Our closets are more likely to be full of old harmonicas and record albums," I said, "but I'll go look."

We have one big walk-in closet upstairs that my mom refuses to go near. It's full of all my dad's old stuff that he won't throw away. There are The Smashing Mozarts posters and boxes of tickets for every rock concert he ever went to and signed albums from bands nobody's ever heard of. Dad thinks maybe he can sell it all for a lot of money on eBay one day, but whenever he says that, Mom goes "Yes, dear," and that's the end of that conversation.

I figured if there were tennis balls anywhere in the house, they'd be in there. And they'd probably be like twenty years old or something. Nobody in my house plays sports except for Isaac's soccer, and I kind of think Mom encourages that to wear him out so he'll be too tired to act crazy at night.

I did find tennis balls in Dad's closet. A can of three was sitting on a shelf next to a set of drumsticks. I thought for a second, and then I took the drumsticks as well. Dad wouldn't mind. He'd be thrilled to think I was interested in anything in his closet. It was actually kind of risky, because I might get stuck listening to some of his Smashing Mozarts music. That's only happened once before, and it was terrible. Poor Dad. It's like nobody ever told him that shouting and singing are two different things.

Outside, Heidi had found Isaac's practice soccer ball and was kicking it around the garden with Trumpet chasing her. I've never been to one of our school's soccer games, but I could tell that Heidi was actually really good. She kept sneaking it away from Trumpet at the last minute and doing these fancy jumps and kicks and footwork to move the ball in new directions.

Trumpet barked and tried to pounce on the ball. Her ears flew up and down. The ball zipped past her and she stopped, turning to the right and left like she couldn't figure out where it had gone. She lowered her head and looked underneath her to see if it was hiding under her legs. Then Heidi made the ball pop up in the air, and Trumpet howl-barked triumphantly, running after it again.

I got to the bottom of the steps just as Trumpet ran under Heidi's feet, and Heidi tripped over the dog and the ball. She crashed to the grass, and Trumpet immediately jumped on her stomach to lick her face.

"This is heaven," Heidi said to me as I came up to her. She laughed and rolled away from Trumpet's tongue. "Literally, when I die, I want to end up in a yard playing with a dog for the rest of eternity."

I sat down on the grass next to her and Trumpet came over to climb into my lap. "I want to be on a stage performing for a huge audience that loves everything I sing." I put down the drumsticks and the tennis balls.

"Gosh, you're brave," Heidi said, sitting up and shaking her head so grass flew everywhere. She had bits of dandelions scattered through her hair. "That's, like, my worst nightmare."

"Really?" I said. I knew Heidi hadn't been in any

of the talent shows, but I thought that was because she couldn't sing or something.

"Performing in front of people?" Heidi said. "I would totally, like, accidentally get tangled in the curtains and make the whole theater collapse. Or fall off the stage. Oh my gosh, that's exactly what I would do. I'd be in the middle of a song and then I'd FALL OFF THE STAGE! Thanks, Ella, my worst nightmare just got much more detailed."

"At least you're not also naked," I offered.

"Aaaah!" Heidi cried, covering her eyes. "I am *so* having that dream tonight! Look what you did!"

"All right, think about Trumpet instead," I said with a smile, popping the lid off the tennis ball can.

"Trumpet would catch me if I fell off the stage naked in front of millions of people, wouldn't you, Trumpet?" Heidi said. Trumpet wagged her tail. She put her front paws on my knee and stretched up to sniff at the tennis-ball can. I handed one of the balls to Heidi.

"Here you go, Trumpet," she said, letting the dog sniff it. "Go get it!" Heidi threw the ball to the other end of the yard.

Trumpet watched it fly through the air and land in a clump of tall grass. Then she looked back at us like, *What'd you do that for?*

"Go on! Fetch!" I said.

Trumpet yawned and scratched behind her ear with her back paw. Heidi giggled.

"I guess she's about as good at fetching as she is at singing," I said. It was weird to be sitting outside in my yard instead of at my piano practicing. Especially with Heidi Tyler, of all people.

"She sings?" Heidi said. "That is so cool! Just like you!"

I shuddered. "Hopefully not just like me."

"Can I hear her?" Heidi asked. "How do you make her sing?"

"The better question is how to make her *stop* singing," I said.

"Ooo, make her do it!" Heidi said.

"OK, but let's go inside, then," I said. "I think the neighbors hate us enough already."

Heidi and Trumpet followed me inside. We stopped in the kitchen for apple juice and then went into the music room. Trumpet immediately jumped into her favorite chair again.

"Wow," Heidi said. "She's totally waiting for you to play. That's hilarious!" She sat down on the black-and-white floor rug that looks like a chess board. Trumpet wagged her tail, but stayed where she was, her eyes focused intently on the piano.

I slid onto the piano bench. I felt kind of weird playing my music for just Heidi. But then, I only had to play a few bars. Once Trumpet started howling, she'd get the idea pretty quickly. I started "Alhambra," and Trumpet immediately flung her head back. She warbled joyfully at the ceiling as I sang. Her eyes were almost closed and she looked like this was the best thing that had ever happened to her in her whole life.

I stopped and turned around. Trumpet kept howling for a second. Then she opened her eyes and cocked her head at me. Like, *Why did you stop? I was just finding my groove!*

"That was so awesome!" Heidi said, clapping and laughing. "Too hilarious! She loves your singing!"

"I'm glad someone does," I said, "but she has a funny way of showing it. Plus it makes it kind of impossible to practice."

"Really?" Heidi said. "She does that every time?"

"Every time!" I said. "I haven't been able to rehearse at home all week."

"Is that what you'd usually be doing now?" she asked. "Rehearsing?"

"Yeah, I do an hour of practice after school and then another hour after dinner," I said. I actually do more than that some days, but I didn't know if Heidi would think that was weird.

"Wow," Heidi said. "I wish I was that good at something. Or that I liked anything enough to spend that much time on it. I mean, I like dogs, but that's not going to win me any awards or anything." Her face lit up. "Hey, maybe if I was playing with Trumpet, she'd let you practice without howling so much."

"Maybe," I said doubtfully.

"Do you want to try?" Heidi offered. "I could take her outside while you play. Unless you don't feel like practicing now."

"I'd love to practice," I admitted. "But you don't have to —"

"That's OK!" Heidi said, jumping to her feet. "It'll be fun! Practice as long as you want! Come on, Trumpet."

Trumpet looked at Heidi, then at me and the piano, then back at Heidi. She slowly stood up and jumped down from the chair, but instead of going to Heidi, she came over to me and pawed at the piano leg.

"Go play with Heidi," I said. "Quietly."

"Here, this might help," Heidi said, pulling

something out of her pocket. It was brown and square. She broke off a piece and held it out to Trumpet.

"What's that?" I asked.

"Um . . . dog treats," she said, blushing.

"You carry dog treats around with you?" I said.

"I know! I'm crazy! I just like dogs!" she said. "I like saying hi to the ones I meet on the street. And I always think maybe I'll find a sad stray who's all alone and then I'll offer him treats and he'll follow me home and we'll live happily ever after. But why would he trust me without treats? So I have to have them with me, just in case."

"Heidi, you really are crazy," I said, but I smiled so she knew I meant it nicely.

"I know," she said, "but it'll be worth it one day."

Trumpet snarfed the treat, wagging her tail, and then followed Heidi out into the yard, keeping her nose as close to Heidi's pocket as she could get. I could see them through the window. Heidi tried throwing the tennis ball again, but Trumpet still didn't get it, so Heidi went back to the soccer ball. Soon they were chasing each other around the yard.

I took a deep breath. I really didn't think this was going to work, but it didn't hurt to try. I started playing "Alhambra" from the beginning again. I was so surprised when I made it all the way to the end of the first line that I stopped and listened. No howling. No barks. Only muffled growls from outside as Trumpet tried to attack the soccer ball. She hadn't even noticed that I was playing.

I kept going and sang the whole song all the way through. Then I did it again, and then I sang "The Last Rose of Summer," and then for good measure I sang all the songs I'd learned in the last year. It was sort of thrilling, like when your favorite TV show comes back after being in reruns all summer and you realize how much you missed all the characters. I felt like myself again.

When I finished the last song I looked at the time. Forty-five minutes had passed. If I were really being good, I should practice for another fifteen. I checked out the window.

Nikos Stavros was in my yard!

I nearly had a heart attack. And then I imagined Tara's face if she knew about this. Miss Bendy Ballerina wouldn't look so pleased then!

Nikos and Heidi were kicking the soccer ball back and forth in the sunshine. Trumpet chased it from one of them to the other. She couldn't get her mouth around it, but she kept trying. Or she would pounce on it with her front paws. When they slipped off and the ball flew away from her, she barked in surprise and chased after it. Sometimes she was able to herd it away from Nikos (who wasn't as good at guarding it as Heidi was), but then Heidi would run after her and kick it back.

Heidi looked up and saw me in the window. She waved, and Nikos looked up, too. I kind of wanted to dart back to the piano, but I waved back. Nikos smiled and motioned for me to come outside.

I was torn. I knew I should practice while I had the chance. And it was much safer to sit inside at the piano instead of going out there. What if I said something stupid in front of Heidi and Nikos? What if they were talking about something I didn't know anything about, like sports or pop music or video games? What if I got out there and then they thought I was boring and wished I'd stayed inside instead?

Avery Lafitte thought I was boring. Tara and Natasha probably did, too. But Trumpet didn't. She finally figured out where Nikos and Heidi were looking. When she spotted me, she barked and wagged her tail like she wanted me to come outside, too.

I closed my piano books and went out into the yard.

CHAPTER 11

I didn't need to worry that Nikos and Heidi would be talking about something like sports. They were talking about Trumpet. Heidi could probably have talked about her for a year and never gotten bored.

"I wonder if she'd like Parker's new dog," Heidi said, dribbling the soccer ball. "Wouldn't it be funny to get them together? Merlin's a lot bigger than Trumpet, but I bet they'd like each other."

I sat down in the shade, and Trumpet came over to me. She flopped down on the lawn right next to me, with her legs sticking straight out behind her. She rested her head between her white front paws. Her long ears lay in velvety folds on the grass. She closed her eyes and sighed contentedly.

"Looks like she's had enough of 'Trumpet in the middle,'" Heidi said.

"We tuckered her out," Nikos said. "Sorry, Ella." His dark hair was all rumpled from running around. It was kind of cute. Not that I noticed.

"No, that's awesome," I said. "A tired Trumpet is a good Trumpet."

He sat down on the grass next to me and then lay down on his back, like this was totally normal, like people came over and hung out in my yard all the time. He put his arms behind his head. "I can't believe *you're* not tired, Heidi," he said.

She grinned, kicked the ball to the other end of the garden, and chased after it.

"It's kind of weird to be out here instead of studying," Nikos said. "Or playing video games."

"I know!" I said. "I feel like I should be inside playing the piano."

"Did you decide what you're going to play for the talent show?" Nikos asked.

"Not yet." I hadn't really had time to think about it. I'd been thinking about Trumpet instead.

Heidi came running up to us. Trumpet opened her eyes and woofed halfheartedly. But she must have decided it would take too much energy to make a bigger fuss, because then she went back to sleep.

"Hey Ella, where'd these come from?" Heidi held up my dad's old drumsticks. I'd forgotten that I had left them next to the tennis ball can.

"I found them in my dad's closet," I said. "You said you liked drums."

"Uh-oh," Nikos said jokingly. "Heidi plus a drum set? Sounds like chaos waiting to happen."

"So totally!" Heidi said, beaming. She sat down, took one in each hand, and started drumming on her thighs. "Ow. OK, I might need to practice on something besides myself."

"You can borrow them," I said. "I'll double-check with Dad." This was another normal-friend thing to do — lend something to someone. It implied that you would hang out with that person again. That you were friends who could trade stuff back and forth. Heidi didn't even think about it.

"Awesome, thank you so much," she said. "I'll bring them back next time I come over." *Next time I come over.* Like there was no question about it.

"Or whenever," I said. See? I can act normal, too. Like we've always been friends like this.

"You are the best dog in the whole world," Heidi said to Trumpet, patting her soft head. Trumpet made a breathy rumbly noise and rolled over so Heidi could rub her stomach.

"She's good when you're here," I said. "It's too bad you can't live here and distract her all the time."

"I *wish*!" Heidi said like she really meant it. "We can trade if you want. My parents would love you."

"If they'll take me to New Zealand, I'll love them,

too," I said. "Or France. Or India. I'm agreeable."
Nikos and Heidi laughed.

"So what do you guys think of Mr. Peary?" Nikos
asked.

And there I was, hanging out in my yard with my
dog and two classmates, talking about normal things —
things like school and TV, instead of symphonies and
minor chords. That's where Mom and Dad found us
an hour later when they got home. Dad's eyebrows
nearly flew off his face.

"Hello, hello!" he said, beaming at Heidi and
Nikos. Nikos looked a little embarrassed. He said
good-bye to us and Trumpet and scooted off to his
own house pretty quickly. I asked Dad about the
drumsticks and he said absolutely Heidi could borrow
them. Then she called her mom and ended up staying
for dinner, and Mom didn't say anything snobby
about music, and Isaac didn't completely cover his
face with food, and Dad didn't sing about the spaghetti, and it was a lot more fun and a lot less disastrous
than I thought it would be.

Plus I saved half a meatball and slipped it into
Trumpet's food dish when Mom wasn't looking. Heidi
saw me do it and gave me a thumbs-up. Trumpet
gobbled it down like she'd never been fed before. Her

tail swished back and forth the whole time she was eating.

After Heidi's mom picked her up, I asked Mom how the will reading had gone. She stopped stacking the dishwasher and sighed. Trumpet snuck up behind her and sniffed the plates that were down at her level. Mom didn't notice.

"There was some kind of legal mix-up with the documents and timelines," she said. "Apparently Golda changed her will just a few months ago, after she got Trumpet, so there were complications. We have to go back again next week for the final details."

"Oh," I said. "So I guess we'll keep Trumpet at least until then, right?" Trumpet had clearly been thinking about licking the plates she could reach, but when she heard her name, she looked up at me and wagged her tail.

"Right," Dad said cheerfully, bringing glasses in from the table.

"But only until then," Mom said. "After that, our lives go back to normal."

Normal for us, that is, which wouldn't look normal at all to anyone else. Then there wouldn't be any reason for Heidi to come over anymore. But I would also be able to get back to practicing. After all, I had my whole future singing career to think about.

I did my homework lying on my bed with Trumpet sprawled out beside me. She was still tired from running around all afternoon. I thought maybe she wouldn't even notice if I put on one of my Sarah Brightman CDs. I was careful not to disturb her as I got off the bed, turned on the stereo, and sat down again. I kept the volume low.

It looked like it might work at first. Trumpet snoozed through the first verse. And then . . . her ears twitched. Her nose twitched. Just as Sarah got to the really romantic part of the song, Trumpet suddenly rolled over, sat up, lifted her nose, and howled soulfully at the top of her lungs.

"Shush," I said, trying to clamp her mouth shut with my hands. That didn't work. She could still make horrible muffled noises. Plus she thought it was a game and tried to lick my hands as I reached for her. Then she tried to chase my hands around the blanket, snuffling and woofing. She trampled all over my math worksheet. She tried to chew on my pencil when I started to write. Probably I shouldn't have bonked her on the nose with it, because then she was *sure* it had to be a toy. And every time Sarah Brightman sang, Trumpet would start to howl. I turned off the music and she snuggled up next to me, putting her head on my lap.

How could a dog be so sweet and so bad at the same time? Why did my whole life have to change if I wanted to keep her?

On Friday, all our teachers made announcements about the talent show being one week away. There was a sign-up sheet posted outside the cafeteria. Danny put his name with Troy's and Hugo's at the top of the list, with "skit" beside it. I heard Mr. Peary tell him he would need to run it by a teacher first. Yumi wrote down "dance." Maggie Olmstead was going to bring her cat and show off what it did in commercials. (I've seen a couple of those commercials. Pretty much the cat sits or stretches or purrs. It's not exactly an Oscar-winning performance. Sorry, Maggie.) Tara put her name and "ballet." Kristal wrote "movie."

My hand shook a little as I wrote down "song" beside my name. I would not let Avery Lafitte scare me away from my calling. He was wrong. He was. He didn't know anything about music. That's what I told myself, but I still kept hearing "BORING!" in my head.

Then it wasn't in my head anymore.

"Oh, *no*," Avery's loud, mean voice said behind

me. "You're going to do *another* whiny song, Finegold? I guess I know when I'll be catching up on my sleep!"

I put the cap back on my pen and shoved it into my pocket without turning around to look at him.

"Cat got your tongue?" Avery said. "Can it keep it until after the talent show?"

I was very close to running away — I was just trying to decide which way to run — when suddenly I felt someone put an arm around my shoulders. The first thing I saw was the untied shoelace on her sneakers, so I knew it was Heidi.

"Avery," Heidi said firmly, "go away."

There was a pause, and then I heard Avery's boots scuffling on the tile as he walked away. Nothing has ever surprised me more in my whole life. It was like Heidi had superpowers or something.

"Don't listen to him," Heidi said to me, shaking my shoulders a little. She squeezed and then let go. "He just wishes he had talent like yours. That's why he's so mean about it. Everyone's jealous of how amazing you are."

"Oh, I'm not — I mean —" I started to say. I still felt like I might be about to cry.

"Whatever!" Heidi said. "You're like our own American Idol! Or something better than that. Man,

I wish I could whip out a real Broadway star's name right now."

"Idina Menzel," I suggested.

"OK, yes. Her," Heidi said. "You're like our own that person."

I laughed, but it came out in a kind of sad gasp. Heidi looked down the hall, saw Tara and Natasha coming, and steered me into the nearest bathroom. "Don't cry," she said. "You shouldn't let Avery make you cry again. He's like, whatever, he's just a guy. He has problems." She grabbed some paper towels and pressed them into my hands.

"Wait," I said, "how do you know Avery has made me cry before?" There was only the one time, after the talent show, and . . . hadn't I been alone in the bathroom?

"Everyone knows," Heidi said. Then she looked guilty. "Didn't you know that? I'm sorry. Cadence heard you. Well, she tried to pretend that she got a message from the universe, but really she was right outside the door. And you know her, she told everyone. But in a nice way! Everyone felt bad. It only made people dislike Avery more."

I could have killed Cadence Bly. It's not fair that someone so gossipy should have such a pretty musical name. Plus she is crazy. She's convinced that she's psychic and she wears these big sunglasses and dangly hoop earrings all the time and she's always telling stories that she says she got by reading people's minds. She was just lucky she was in Miss Woodhull's class and I couldn't, like, stab her to death with a violin bow.

At least being mad meant I didn't feel like crying anymore. "Well, that's embarrassing," I said.

"Not as embarrassing as pretty much my entire life," Heidi said. "And you're not the only one. Avery made fun of Maggie's cat and she was *so* upset." I felt a twinge of guilt for making fun of Maggie's cat, too . . . but at least I only did it in my head!

After school I had another lesson with Mrs. Mehta. She tried to help me choose between the two songs for the talent show.

"'Alhambra' is very pretty," she said. "It's sort of unusual and exotic. I would think the judges would like that."

"Yeah, maybe," I said. Lip-synching to Hannah Montana wasn't exactly unusual and exotic. I wasn't sure the judges would like either of these songs, now that I really had to decide. I wasn't sure the audience would like them either.

"But 'The Last Rose of Summer' is terribly sweet," Mrs. Mehta said. "And appropriate for the end of summer and the beginning of the school year. Is that what you're thinking?"

Actually, I was thinking about whether I could learn a Miley Cyrus song in under a week. But I smiled at Mrs. Mehta and said, "Yeah, I'm just not sure. Neither one feels right yet. I'll keep practicing and think about it." Except how was I supposed to practice over the weekend with Trumpet around?

"I wish Pradesh loved music as much as you do, Ella," Mrs. Mehta said, shaking her head. "Thank goodness for my talented little Kamala!" She smiled fondly at her daughter, who was sitting at the kitchen table, doing her homework. Kamala beamed back. I felt kind of bad for Pradesh. My mom would never say something like that about me and Isaac.

"Well, at least Pradesh is good at lots of other things," I pointed out. "You know, like spelling. Unlike Isaac, who hates music and is also the biggest brat in the world."

Kamala giggled. "I can spell, too, you know," she said.

"Come here and play your piece for Ella before she leaves," Mrs. Mehta said.

Kamala didn't sing along with her piece, but it was very pretty and complicated for a nine-year-old. It made me wish I had a little sister who could play duets with me, instead of dopey, irritating Isaac.

That night after dinner I sat down at the piano. Trumpet jumped onto her chair and waited. Her tongue hung sideways out of her mouth as she panted and grinned. Her ears hung down like big cymbals on either side of her head.

After a minute, when I just sat there without playing, she jumped down and trotted over. She touched the piano leg with one paw and looked at me.

"What's the point?" I said. "You're not going to let me practice."

She stuck her nose under the piano and snuffled at the pedals. Her whiskers tickled my bare feet. I peeked down and saw her stand on one of the pedals. She sniffed up and down the bottom of the piano. Then she wriggled her way out again backward. She sat down and looked up at me with very serious brown eyes.

"Oh, Trumpet," I said. "Why can't you just be good?"

Trumpet stood up and came over to rest her chin on the piano bench beside me. It was a little too high for her, so it looked really silly, the way she had to stick her head in the air to reach it. After a second, she sat down again, then stood up and put her front paws up on the bench beside me.

"Sure," I said, patting the bench. "It's not like I can play either way."

Trumpet hoisted herself up beside me and stood there sniffing the piano keys. She put one paw tentatively on the keyboard and then leaned forward to sniff the top of the piano. *BLAAAT!* went the keys under her paw. She jumped back and nearly slipped off the bench, but I caught her.

"I don't know what to do, Trumpet," I said, keeping my arms around her. "The talent show is one week away. I don't know what to sing, I don't have time to practice, and I'm afraid it's going to be boring anyway."

She lifted her nose and licked my chin. Which didn't really solve my problems . . . but at least I felt a little better.

CHAPTER 12

The doorbell woke me up on Saturday morning. I realized it was already ten o'clock. It was weird for Mom to let me sleep that late. Even Trumpet was still asleep, although she came wriggling out from under the bed when she heard the doorbell. She bounded over to my bedroom door and barked. And barked. And barked.

I pulled my musical-note comforter over my head. Someone else would answer the door. Someone not in their cow pajamas.

"Ella!" my mom's voice called from downstairs. She said something else, but I couldn't hear her over Trumpet's barking.

"Shush!" I said to Trumpet. "Trumpet! Shut up!"

But finally I had to get up and open the door for her. Trumpet bolted down the stairs. I heard her barking her way into the living room, and then she got quiet, except for the jingling of her collar, which meant she was probably wagging her tail and getting petted.

I got dressed quickly, just in case — not that I thought it would be Nikos, but I'd already made that mistake once! — and followed the dog down the stairs, yawning.

"Ella, look who's here," Mom said as I poked my head into the living room.

Heidi bounced to her feet. "I'm sorry!" she said. "I'm sorry, I know it's early and I should have called first but this morning I knocked a picture frame off the wall and broke it and then I was trying to make pancakes but I forgot to put the lid on the blender and now there are bananas all over my kitchen and so I kind of had to get out of the house and I thought maybe I could come over here and maybe Mom would have forgotten how much she wants to kill me by the time I get home." She made a *please forgive me please* scrunched-up face.

I was still stuck back at "pancakes" and "blender," and I think my mom was, too. She looked confused.

"Um, that's OK," I said.

"And so I thought maybe I could distract Trumpet some more and you could practice," Heidi said. "If you want. Only if you want. Or I could go home. If you're busy. Are you busy?"

"No, no," my mom said. Her eyes lit up. I'd told her about Heidi keeping Trumpet distracted. My mom loved this plan. Anything to help me practice. "We're having bagels for breakfast, if you'd like one. Or did you eat already?"

"No," Heidi said ruefully. Her hair was covered with a light dusting of flour and had a couple of raisins stuck in it.

"Well, you're welcome to stay as long as you like," Mom said, and bustled off to the kitchen.

Heidi looked at me and started giggling. "I like your hair," she said.

"*My* hair!" I said, pressing down my crazy curls. "Have you seen *your* hair?"

Heidi went over to a mirror on the wall. She clapped her hands to her face and started laughing. "I biked over here like this!" she said. "The neighbors must think I escaped from an asylum or something."

"An asylum for crazy bakers," I said. I helped her rescue the raisins from her hair.

"I'm sorry I woke you," she said.

"No, it's OK, I'm glad you're here," I said. "I was wondering how I'd get time this weekend to practice for the talent show."

"Oh yeah!" Heidi said excitedly. "I can help with that! Right, Trumpet?"

Trumpet barked and ran in a circle around us, as if she was saying *I love this plan too! I love it! It's brilliant! Whatever you said! More treats!*

So after breakfast, Heidi took Trumpet outside with the soccer ball again.

"I want to play soccer, too!" Isaac yelled.

"Honey, don't bother the girls," Mom said.

"It's OK if he wants to," Heidi said. "It's easier to tire Trumpet out with two people. And then it'll be like we're training." She smiled at Isaac and he grinned back. See, I told you — superpowers. Like Heidi can tame anything, even annoying little brothers.

I practiced my two songs while they played outside, but I had trouble concentrating. I could hear Isaac shrieking whenever the ball flew past him, but that wasn't what was distracting me. I felt like nothing would be right for the talent show. I tried some of my old songs. I listened to Charlotte Church's album. I just couldn't imagine singing these songs in front of my school anymore.

Heidi came back in after an hour and collapsed on the rug in the music room. Trumpet went over to the chair and stood there for a moment like Aunt Miriam's Pekingese, panting and staring thoughtfully at the cushion like it was just too hard to jump up. Then she went back to Heidi and flopped down with her head on one of Heidi's outstretched arms. I turned around on the piano bench to face them.

"I feel much better," Heidi said. "Thanks, Ella." Which was funny, because she was totally the one doing *me* a favor. She was all hot and sweaty from running around. It didn't look like fun to me. She put one hand on her stomach, taking deep breaths to cool down.

"Wow," I said, "look how exhausted Trumpet is. That's hilarious."

Heidi smiled and rolled sideways to pet Trumpet's head. Trumpet snuffled but didn't even open her eyes.

"Maybe she'll even sleep through you singing," Heidi said. "Can I hear what you're going to sing for the talent show?"

"Oh . . . I haven't decided yet, actually." I picked up some sheet music and shuffled it in my hands. This one? This one? What would win?

"Maybe I can help!" Heidi said.

"OK — are you sure?" I said. "You won't be bored?"

"Are you kidding?" she said. "I loved that song you did last year. I wish I were talented like you."

"Well, I wish I went to New Zealand this summer, like you," I said. "And I'm only good at this one thing. I'm terrible at other stuff."

"I'm terrible at everything!" Heidi said. "Except soccer, I guess. When I focus."

"See, sports is a good example," I said. "I'm terrible at sports. Anything involving my feet is a disaster. Mom made me take ballet this summer and I learned that (a) pink is not my color, (b) leotards are evil, and (c) my feet point in one direction and one direction only."

"I took ballet, too!" Heidi cried. "Two summers ago. I was awful! In my third class I leaned on the barre too hard and it broke! All the ballerinas came crashing down! They kicked me out after that. Mercifully."

"Was Tara in your class?" I asked.

"Oh, yeah," Heidi said with a shudder. "People really shouldn't be able to bend that way. It's unnatural." She lay down on her back again and closed her eyes. "Go ahead and play. I'm listening. And if a certain someone tries to sing along, I'll sit on her until she stops."

"All right," I said. "This one is called 'The Last Rose of Summer.'" I sang it all the way through, and Trumpet didn't make a peep.

"You should do that one," Heidi said when I finished. "That was amazing."

"Or there's this one, 'Alhambra.'" I said. Again I made it all the way through without an off-key interruption. I was completely astonished. If we could just tire out Trumpet like this every morning, she might be a really good dog.

"Oooh, do that one," Heidi said. "I loved that one!"

"Really?" I said. "Better than the first one? Are you sure?"

"I don't know, it's hard," she said. She sat up, wriggling her arm out from under Trumpet's head, and tapped her fingers together. "They're both pretty. It's too bad the judges always go for funny instead, you know? Because if they were really looking for talent, you'd win every time, hands down."

"I really want to win this year," I said. That would show Avery! "You think these won't win?"

"I don't know," Heidi said. "Maybe . . . do you know any funny songs?"

"My voice teacher doesn't like funny songs," I said. "But — hang on." I got off the piano bench. Trumpet opened her eyes and watched me hurry out of the room like she wished she had the energy to follow me.

I went to my dad's closet and turned on the light

inside. I knew which file box to look in because it's the same one where he keeps the songbooks we use at Passover, when he likes to play the piano and make everyone sing along. His other piano books were in the box, too. I pulled out a whole stack of them and brought them downstairs.

Heidi's eyes widened. "Your secret stash!" she cried. "You keep happy songs hidden in your closet! I knew it!"

I laughed. "Actually, it's my dad's secret stash of happy songs." I sat down on the floor beside her and gave her half the stack. "I bet there's something in here I could learn by Friday."

Heidi picked up the first book. "Ella Fitzgerald!" she said. "I've heard of her!"

"That's who I'm named after," I said.

"Ooooohhhh," Heidi said. "That makes sense. I never knew that." She flipped to the table of contents. "'Summertime' . . . 'Our Love Is Here to Stay' . . . 'Let's Call the Whole Thing Off' . . ."

"Oh, that one's funny," I said. "Here, let me try it." I took the songbook and put it up on the piano. The song was actually a duet, but the piano part wasn't too complicated. Plus I'd heard it before, so I knew how it should go. I read through the music, touching the keys lightly.

The version I've heard is Ella singing with Louis Armstrong, who has this deep, gravelly voice. So when I began playing, I did half the song in my regular voice and half in my best Louis Armstrong imitation. Heidi started laughing as soon as I busted that out. At the end they sing together so I kind of had to fancy my way around it. I hit the last notes with a flourish.

Heidi was laughing too hard to talk for a minute. "That was crazy!" she said when she could breathe again. "Have you really never played that before?"

"Well, this is an easy version," I said.

"Ella, you're so funny! You have to do something like that. The judges will die! Everyone would love it!"

I remembered Parker in the music room at school telling me I was funny, too. I couldn't remember that happening before, although Dad always laughs at my jokes. But twice in one week — maybe it was a sign from the universe. Maybe I could find something easy enough to learn in a week . . . something that the judges would like, that would definitely not be boring.

Something that would finally help me win the talent show.

CHAPTER 13

Mom was impressed when she found me playing the piano with Trumpet snoozing peacefully on the floor beside us.

"See, maybe she's not so bad," I said.

"Don't you start, too," Mom said. "Lunch is almost ready, girls." She went back to the kitchen.

Heidi gave me a puzzled look. "What did that mean?"

"Mom wants to get rid of Trumpet," I admitted. Heidi gasped.

"But why? You just got her! And — and she's perfect!"

Trumpet opened her eyes and furrowed her brow and gave us the most perfectly mournful look.

"I know, I guess — Mom's just worried about my music and all the noise — she thinks it's disrupting our lives."

"Oh, don't let them give you away!" Heidi said,

throwing her arms around Trumpet. Trumpet blinked at me like, *Why is someone lying on me right now?*

"Let me help!" Heidi said. "I'll come over every day if you want. It's only like ten minutes by bike. I wouldn't mind!"

"I wouldn't either," I said. That kind of surprised me. I'd gone from being afraid of Heidi Tyler to kind of wanting her around all the time — in three days! "But you have soccer practice and stuff, or you might be on vacation — it's too crazy."

"We'll find a solution," Heidi said. "I have every episode of *The Dog Whisperer* and *It's Me or the Dog* saved on my TV. We can train her not to howl, I know we can! Dogs are amazing that way!"

I shrugged doubtfully. "We can try," I said.

Boy, was that the wrong thing to say. Heidi went home after lunch, but she came back again on Sunday morning with a pile of books.

"Look what I found in the library!" she said as soon as I opened the door. She waved the top book at me while Trumpet jumped around her feet. "Dog training! Perfect puppies! And I checked it out online, too. Did you know beagles are famous for howling so much?"

"Oh, terrific," I said. "See, Trumpet, you're more normal than you thought."

"We should start with some basic commands,"

Heidi said, leading the way into the music room and dumping the books on the rug. "Do you have any treats? I brought mine, but if you have more, we can use them. Or cheese or turkey or something."

I left her with Trumpet and went into the kitchen, where Dad was mixing pancake batter in a big blue plastic bowl.

"This is great!" Dad said with a huge smile. "Heidi seems like a great, great girl. It's great to meet your friends."

"Wait, so, do you think it's great, or not?" I asked.

"Really great," Dad said again.

"We're going to work on training Trumpet for a while," I said, opening the refrigerator. "Can I use these leftover meatballs?"

"Sure!" Dad said. "But, um, maybe tell your mom that I ate them." He winked at me.

I took the Tupperware container into the music room. Heidi was sitting on the floor surrounded by open books. Trumpet was standing on one of them with her nose down on the page. It looked kind of like she was reading it, except the book was upside down.

Trumpet sat bolt upright when I took the lid off the Tupperware. She could definitely smell the meatballs. She got up on her hind legs and stuck her nose up as high in the air as she could get it, sniffing and twitching it.

"Oh, perfect," Heidi said, clapping her hands. "Look how excited she is. That means she's probably very food-motivated."

"What does that mean?" I asked.

"I read about this last night. It means she'll do anything for food," Heidi said importantly.

"Aha," I said. "Like Isaac."

Heidi laughed and climbed to her feet. "Well, it should make her easier to train, so maybe you should try this technique on him, too. Let's start with the regular treats first." I closed the container again, and Heidi held out a dog treat in front of Trumpet's nose. Trumpet jumped for it and Heidi pulled it away.

"Sit," Heidi said.

Trumpet stared at her, wagging her tail. Her face said *Dude, give me that treat. I know you don't want it.*

"My dad tried this, too," I said, "but it didn't work so well. He had to kind of push her butt down to make her sit."

Heidi glanced at the book. "That's not the best way. OK, you're supposed to move it over their nose like this." She stepped toward Trumpet and held the treat over the dog's head. Trumpet raised her nose toward it — farther and farther back as Heidi moved it slowly. As Trumpet's head went up, her butt slowly went down. Until, suddenly, Trumpet was sitting!

"Good girl!" Heidi said happily, giving Trumpet the treat. "Good sit! Good dog!"

"That was so logical," I marveled. "Like if she's following the treat, it's just easier for her to sit down, so of course she did."

"Exactly," Heidi said. "Here, you try." She tossed me a treat.

I called Trumpet to me. Trumpet had seen the treat fly through the air so she came right over and stood in front of me, her eyes fixed on the treat in my hand. I did the same thing Heidi had done. I moved the treat over her head and said "sit" firmly. Trumpet's nose went up. Her butt went down. She was sitting! I made her sit!

"Yay!" Heidi squealed.

"Good dog!" I said to Trumpet. "Whoever thought you'd hear that?" Trumpet was as excited as we were. She jumped to her feet and barked and wagged her tail like crazy. I was amazed. Maybe there really was hope for Trumpet after all.

We practiced that until breakfast was ready. We each took turns calling Trumpet over and making her sit. Heidi showed me a hand signal that was supposed to help. While you held the treat in one hand, you were supposed to hold the other hand flat, palm up.

She said dogs often learned the hand signals before they figured out the words.

"Depending on how smart they are and how they learn best," Heidi said. "Of course, Trumpet is a genius, so she'll have it down in no time."

"A genius," I said to Trumpet. "You hear that? You should appreciate Heidi for believing in you." Trumpet wagged her tail like, *I do! I do! I AM a genius!*

Dad couldn't stop grinning at us all through breakfast. Seriously, I had no idea he thought I was so friendless. He didn't really know Caroline or any of my music-camp friends. I would have tried a lot harder to bring someone home before if I knew he'd get so excited about it. Like, I always knew my mom had big dreams about my music. I just didn't know that my dad also had such lofty goals for me, like "have friends over for pancakes."

"Your father tells me you girls have been playing with Trumpet this morning," Mom said to me. I could hear a hint of disapproval in her voice, but Heidi missed it completely.

"We're training her!" Heidi said happily. "By the time we're done, she's going to be the best dog in the world! Wait and see. She won't howl or anything."

"Hmmm," Mom said.

"I want to play soccer with Trumpet!" Isaac shouted suddenly. "I want to play with her! I want —"

"Here, Isaac, have some of my pancake," I said, cutting off a corner and dropping it on his plate, which he had practically licked clean already.

Isaac's eyes went very wide. "Really?" he said and then dove on it before I could change my mind. His mouth being full made the table quiet again. I raised my eyebrows at Heidi. Her shoulders were shaking with laughter. I had to look away quickly, or I'd have started laughing, too, and then Isaac or Mom and Dad might have figured out that I was using a dog trick on him.

"Don't you want to take Trumpet outside after breakfast?" Mom asked Heidi as Dad collected the plates. "Then perhaps Ella could practice for a little while . . ."

"Glenda," my dad said in a warning voice.

"She *is* going to practice!" Heidi said. "That's step two of the training. We're going to make Trumpet be quiet while Ella sings."

"Well," Mom said skeptically, "that would be nice."

Once we were back in the music room, Heidi said, "You know, I think your mom might be more like my mom than I realized." So perhaps she did pick up on some of the disapproval.

"She just needs to warm up to Trumpet," I said, burying my hands in the dog's fur. "She's never had a dog before."

"Me neither," Heidi said. "But I'm ready for one! I really am!"

"Maybe we can convince her," I said. "Let's try part two of the training."

Heidi explained her plan to me. The idea was to distract Trumpet before she started singing along with me. Heidi was hoping that she could get Trumpet to focus on her and food while I sang, so she'd be quiet.

"This is going to take more than regular treats," Heidi said. "This is going to require . . . meatballs!"

Trumpet leaped to her feet again when she saw me reach for the Tupperware. She actually remembered the smell that had come from there. She stared at the container with laser intensity. Heidi took it and led Trumpet across the room. I sat down at the piano and played a chord. Trumpet glanced back at me, but then Heidi opened the Tupperware, and Trumpet's head whipped around toward her.

"Sit," Heidi said, making the hand signal. I kept playing. Trumpet sat and got a piece of meatball. "Go ahead," Heidi whispered. I started to sing.

Trumpet was definitely torn. She took a few steps toward me, lifting her head and squeak-growling a little. But Heidi waved another piece of meatball at her, and Trumpet caved. She hurried back to Heidi's feet and sat down.

We were able to get through a whole song like that, although it cost us almost all the meatballs.

"Well, it's something," Heidi said cheerfully. "Hopefully, eventually she'll be able to sit and focus for longer and longer, and then you can make her sit for a whole song, totally quietly, just so she can get a reward at the end."

"That'll be a miracle," I said.

"So what about the talent show?" Heidi asked. "Have you chosen a song?"

"Well . . . I have an idea," I said slowly. "I thought of it last night, going through Dad's old stuff. But it's kind of crazy." It wasn't like anything I'd ever done before. But nothing I'd done before had ever won. Maybe it was time to try something new.

"I love crazy!" Heidi interjected.

"And I kind of need some help with it."

"I can help!" Heidi said right away. Trumpet barked, like she was saying *I want to help, too!*

"Are you sure?" I said to Heidi. "Even if it means being on stage?"

Heidi went a little pale. She wound a strand of strawberry-blond hair around her finger. "Um . . . tell me more," she said.

"We're also going to need another girl," I said.

"Do you know anyone who would want to perform with us? Preferably someone who can sing a little."

"Rory," Heidi said promptly. "She's always wanted to be in the talent show, but she can never think of anything to do. She'd be all over this."

"Really?" I said. "Rory Mason? In the talent show?" I didn't think Rory Mason was interested in anything but sports. She's a lot like Heidi, but shorter and louder and bossier and totally fearless. I heard that last summer she skateboarded off the top of the library steps on a dare and broke her leg. And in fourth grade she did cartwheels all the way down the hall and got yanked into Vice Principal Taney's office. That was also on a dare. I guess we could have dared her to be in the talent show. Then she'd definitely do it.

"I've heard her sing," Heidi said. "We had a karaoke slumber party once at Virginia's house. She's really good! I mean, obviously not as good as you, but I bet you'd be surprised."

I *would* be surprised. I didn't think someone could be good at sports *and* singing. But if Heidi thought it was a good idea . . .

"OK," I said, "let's ask her."

I brought Heidi the portable telephone and she dialed Rory's number. She knew it by heart, which made me realize that they must hang out a lot. I hoped Heidi would still be my friend, even with Rory around. I hoped they wouldn't laugh at me like Tara and Natasha.

"Rory!" Heidi said into the phone. "Whatcha doing? Oh, I should have guessed that." She looked at me. "Rory's playing catch with her dad. Of course! What?" she said back into the phone. "Oh, I'm with Ella. We're playing with her dog. I know! You have to meet her! She's the cutest thing! I mean Trumpet, not you," she said to me. "I mean, you're cute, too, but Trumpet wins. What? Well, that's why I'm calling, knucklehead. We want you to come over. Ella has an idea for the talent show. No, for all of us! I know! It *is* exciting! Get your butt over here!" Heidi told her my address.

It turned out Rory's house was only a couple of streets away. It wasn't even ten minutes later when the doorbell rang and Trumpet went berserk. She and Heidi and I ran out to the living room, but my mom was already opening the door.

Rory was on the front steps, panting. She looked like she had run all the way over. Her long, straight brown hair was pulled back in a ponytail under a dark blue baseball cap with a red B on it. She was wearing a red tank top, khaki shorts, and sneakers. She looked like she had just hurtled out of some kids' sports magazine. I don't know if they have those, but if they do, Rory should be on the front cover.

Trumpet threw herself at Rory's legs, barking and wagging her tail. Rory crouched down and went, "Oh man! Adorable! Hey buddy!" She tugged lightly on Trumpet's ears and Trumpet jumped up to lick her face.

Mom blinked a lot like she was startled. Girls like Rory don't usually appear on our doorstep. I could sense that she was about to tell Rory that we already bought all our Girl Scout cookies or something.

"Mom, this is Rory," I blurted quickly. "She's here to meet Trumpet." I wasn't sure yet what Mom would think of my talent-show plan. I was afraid she wouldn't like it.

"Oh," my mom said. "Oh, that's — well, lovely —"

"It's great!" my dad interrupted, bounding into the room. "Nice to meet you! Come on in! Have you eaten breakfast? We have some pancakes left over."

"Thanks, I'm all good," Rory said. She stood up again and Trumpet immediately tried to jump up into her arms.

"We'll be in the music room," I said quickly. "Trumpet, come on!"

"All right," Mom said, "but don't forget you need to practice, Ella — the talent show is on Friday."

"That's what we're —" Rory started to say.

"I remember!" I shouted over her. "Got it! No problem! Thanks, Mom!" I grabbed Rory's arm,

Heidi grabbed the other, and we dragged her off to the music room before she could say anything else. Trumpet chased after us, barking with excitement.

"OK," Rory said, rubbing her head as I flung the door shut behind us. "Confused."

Trumpet sprawled out on the rug, panting and looking very pleased with herself. Her white paws and brown patches glowed in the sunshine pouring through the windows.

"It's a surprise for Ella's mom and dad," Heidi said. "They don't know what we're doing. Then again, I don't know what we're doing either."

"Hey, this is cool," Rory said, looking around. "You really do have a music room. I thought that was only in, like, old mansions and stuff. Whoa, check out all these albums." She picked up a Shangri-Las single from the top of the stack of my dad's albums. I'd brought them down last night and put them on the bookcase. "This is really old!"

"Tell us your idea, Ella!" Heidi begged. "I'm dying to hear it."

"Yeah, totally," Rory said. She sat down on the floor and rubbed Trumpet's stomach. Trumpet's tail thumped on the floor.

"Well, you remember what won last year, right?" I said.

"No," Rory said. "I thought you won. Didn't you? You were the best."

"Yeah, but it was Delia and her friends doing that Hannah Montana song, right?" Heidi said.

"Exactly," I said, "and they weren't even really singing. They were lip-synching. So we're going to do something like that, but even better, because we'll be really singing."

"Uh-oh," Heidi said. "That counts me out."

"No, wait till you hear it," I said. "It's going to be really funny. Hang on, though; we don't have enough meatballs for this, so I gotta get rid of Trumpet first. Just for a minute." I took one of Heidi's treats and lured Trumpet out of the room behind me. She trotted happily up to Isaac's room with me.

"Isaac?" I said, knocking on the door. He was sitting at his desk, playing a game on his computer. His floor was covered in trucks and clothes and action figures and sneakers and crumpled magazines. His soccer sheets were shoved to the bottom of his bed and his pillows were both on the floor. One of his posters was coming unstuck from the wall and drooping toward the floor. The room looked like Bigfoot had been living in it for the last year.

"Private! No trespassing!" he yelled as I stuck my head in. "No girls allowed!"

"But Trumpet's a girl," I pointed out. Trumpet trotted into the room happily and started poking her nose into the piles of dirty laundry on the floor.

"Well — but —" Isaac sputtered.

"You wanna play with her outside?" I asked.

He squinted at me. "No."

"But you did before!" I said. "You can have her now! All to yourself! You guys can play soccer!"

Isaac crossed his arms. "Maybe I don't want to anymore," he said.

"Isaac!" I stamped my foot. "You are *so* annoying!"

"*You're* so annoying!" he yelled.

Of course, that brought Dad out of his room. "What's going on in here?" he demanded.

"I was just offering to let Isaac play with Trumpet for a while," I said sweetly.

"She just wants me to keep the dog busy!" Isaac said. "She's not really being nice!"

"I wouldn't mind playing some soccer," Dad said. "I was going to mow the lawn, but playing with Trumpet sounds like a lot more fun. Oh, well, too bad you don't want to join us, Isaac."

Isaac perked up. "Wait — I'll play if you're playing."

"No, no," Dad said. "We wouldn't want to interrupt what you're doing. I'll just go hang out with Trumpet by myself."

"I'll come!" Isaac shouted. "I want to!" He dove into a pile of laundry, digging for his shoes. Trumpet thought this was a wonderful game and tried to help by digging alongside him. She found one of his socks and shook it ferociously. Isaac tried to grab it away and soon there was a sock tug-of-war going on.

"Thanks, Dad," I whispered. He gave me a thumbs-up, and I hurried back to Rory and Heidi.

Once we were sure Trumpet was distracted outside, I told them my idea. First I played them the original song, which I had downloaded from the Internet. Then I played it on the piano and told them which parts they would do and how it would look. Then I told them the final piece — the part that would bring it all together and make it the funniest talent-show performance ever.

My heart was going really fast. "What do you think?" I asked. I had this terrible feeling they would hate it. I was afraid they would say, "That's stupid," and leave. I imagined them telling everyone at school how dumb I was and what terrible ideas I had.

Heidi started laughing. "I *love* it!" she said. "That's the best thing I've ever heard!"

"Me too!" Rory said. "Wow, I'm going to be in the talent show! Finally!"

"And we're going to win!" Heidi cried, pumping her hands in the air.

CHAPTER 14

The hardest part was keeping our plan a secret. I knew it would only be funny if people weren't expecting it. So Heidi and Rory and I swore ourselves to secrecy. Even when Nikos asked me at school on Monday whether I'd picked a song to do, I just smiled and said, "I'm working on it."

I did tell Mrs. Mehta at my lesson, though, because I wanted her help with the piano part. It wasn't very difficult in the book I had, but I wanted to make sure I was doing it right and I thought I could change a couple of things to make it sound cooler. She was really surprised by my choice.

"This is quite unlike you, Ella," she said. "You're sure you wouldn't rather do 'Alhambra'?"

"I'm sure," I said. "I think this'll be fun. But don't tell my parents, OK? I want to surprise them."

"Oh, they'll be surprised," Mrs. Mehta said.

I was lucky Kamala wasn't there to hear me practice the song. I had a feeling she couldn't keep a secret.

Pradesh might have heard me playing from upstairs, but he didn't come out and he didn't say anything about it later. I was pretty sure he wasn't really interested.

On Tuesday afternoon I went over to Heidi's so we could practice. Her family had a piano in what her mother called the "company room." That meant that her parents usually only used that room when they had fancy guests. Everything in it was very clean and very white and very delicate-looking. Heidi seemed terrified the whole time we were in there. She didn't want to move too much in case she knocked something over. She stood very still right in the center of the rug, practically holding her breath. Her mother seemed to have the same worry, because she kept walking by the doorway. We could tell she was trying to watch us without being too obvious about it.

So on Thursday we went to Rory's to practice, even though Rory didn't have a piano; she only had a Casio keyboard. But it was enough to practice with. We went through the song over and over again. I was surprised that Heidi and Rory didn't mind how much I wanted to practice it.

Heidi might even have wanted to practice more than I did. She was really afraid of doing it wrong. I caught her in the hall at school on Thursday doing the motions and muttering the words.

"Heidi, don't worry!" I said. "It's only a few lines. You'll be awesome."

"Easy for you to say," she said. "I bet you've never fallen off a stage in your life."

"Neither have you, and you're not going to start tomorrow night," I said. "Besides, Rory will catch you if you start to teeter. You know how strong she is."

"That's true!" Heidi said.

And after rehearsing, Rory and Heidi came over and walked Trumpet with me. This helped Heidi relax. She liked to take Trumpet's leash and race ahead down the street with Trumpet at her heels, barking and yipping.

We also kept working on Trumpet's training. By Friday, she could sit *and* stay for a whole three minutes. She wasn't exactly perfect about not singing, however. I still had to give her a treat every thirty seconds if I wanted her to shut up while I sang.

I wasn't worried about that yet, though. First I would make it through the talent show. Then I'd focus on training Trumpet really well.

My mom came into my room Thursday night. I was in bed reading *Shiloh,* which Mr. Peary had decided was an acceptable substitute for *Old Yeller.* Trumpet was curled up next to me. She had her nose buried in the little space between my back and the pillow. Her ears were flopped back inside out. Sometimes her paws twitched in her sleep, and she made whuffling growling noises like she was dreaming about chasing a soccer ball.

Mom raised her eyebrows a little when she saw Trumpet on the bed, but she didn't say anything about it. Instead she sat down on the bed next to me. Trumpet's ear twitched, but she kept sleeping.

"Are you ready for the talent show?" Mom asked. "I feel like I haven't heard you play in days."

"I have been playing," I said. "I practiced at Heidi's and Rory's houses, and with Mrs. Mehta. I'm ready." I tugged on a bit of feather that was sticking out of my comforter. "I hope you like it, Mom."

"Of course I will, sweetie," Mom said. "I liked both songs when I heard you play them before."

"I'm not doing one of those songs," I said. "I'm doing something different."

"Oh," Mom said. "Really? What is it?"

"It's a surprise," I said.

"Oh," Mom said again, smoothing out a wrinkle on my pillow. "Well, I'm sure I'll like it."

"Mom," I said, "I want to keep Trumpet."

"Oh, dear," Mom said. She took off her glasses and rubbed them with her shirt. "I was afraid of this."

"She's not really a bad dog," I said. "She means to be good." I patted Trumpet's back. Trumpet wriggled around so her paws flopped onto my leg and I could scratch her belly. "I promise to keep training her and I promise I'll still practice and I know she can be a good dog and — and I really like her."

"Hrrrmmmmwrrrrooooo," Trumpet agreed sleepily.

"I'm just worried about how distracted you've been," Mom said. "I don't want anything to get in the way of your music."

"She won't," I said. "I know she won't. Great-Aunt Golda wouldn't have left her to me if she thought it was a bad idea, right?"

"Let me think about it," Mom said. "I really don't know if this family can handle the chaos that comes with having a dog."

"I think we can," I said. "I'll help. I'll do whatever."

"Well, we're meeting with the lawyers about the will again tomorrow. So we'll see," Mom said. Which was ominous. "We'll see" usually means "No, we aren't going to Disney World this summer" and "No, you can't get a second piercing in your ear" and "No, because we said so."

I just had to hope that our performance at the talent show would change her mind. Once she saw what I could do — once she saw that I wasn't distracted, that I could still do my music — once I *won* the talent show . . . maybe then she'd agree to keep Trumpet.

CHAPTER 15

I always have butterflies before a performance, but on Friday they felt more like giant hedgehogs rolling around in my stomach. I was so nervous. There were so many things that could go wrong. Starting with Heidi falling off the stage and ending with nobody laughing at our song. That would be the worst. I was horribly afraid that it wouldn't be funny, and then Parker would think he was wrong about me being hilarious, and Nikos would stop wanting to hang out with us, and Tara and Natasha would smirk and whisper, and, of course, Avery would say something hurtful and horrible. That thought kept rattling around and around in my head. *What if we weren't funny?*

It was actually a relief to see that Heidi was as nervous as I was. The only one who wasn't scared was Rory. Like I said before, she's not afraid of anything. She couldn't wait to get up on that stage.

"Three more hours!" she said, bouncing from foot to foot and punching the air in front of her like a boxer. School had just ended and we were standing next to Heidi's locker, watching Heidi try to get one of her textbooks out without setting off an avalanche of stuff. The talent show was scheduled for six o'clock.

Tara was across the hall at her locker. She picked up one of her feet and stretched it way over her head in a long split. Then she did a couple of weird bendy things with her arms and legs. It looked like she was just stretching to warm up, but I was pretty sure she was trying to freak us out. I hate to admit it, but it was kind of impressive. Would the judges like her ballet better than our piece?

Then I saw Nikos coming down the hall toward us. He was wearing a warm brown T-shirt that was kind of the same color as Trumpet. Maybe Tara was showing off for him. That wouldn't be surprising. But he didn't even look at her. Instead he came straight over to us. And he smiled at me. He really did! Not that that meant anything. But I could tell that Tara had noticed.

"Hey guys," Nikos said. He leaned on the locker next to Heidi's. "Are you ready for the run-through?"

"The run-through?" Heidi said, and then dove for a pile of books as they all came sliding out of her locker. I clapped my hand to my mouth.

"I forgot about that!" I said. "We're supposed to run through the whole show for the teacher supervisors before tonight. I can't believe I didn't remember!"

"Yeah, I think you're supposed to be in the auditorium in about twenty minutes," Nikos said, checking his watch. He knelt down and helped Heidi shove the runaway books back into her locker. She slammed it shut quickly to keep them in there. I made a mental note not to be standing in the way next time she opened it again.

"Uh-oh," Rory said. "What about the surprise? How will we keep it secret?"

"Surprise?" Nikos echoed curiously. "What surprise?"

"I thought I'd have time to go home and come back!" I said.

"Maybe Nikos can help," Heidi said. She looked around at all the other kids in the hallway, some of whom were close enough to hear us. Tara was still bending herself into freaky shapes, but I was pretty sure she was listening. Heidi lowered her voice. "Maybe he can *get what we need*." She gave us all a wide-eyed, meaningful expression.

"Sure," Nikos said. "What can I do?"

"Use my cell phone," Rory said, digging it out of her pocket.

I glanced at Tara. "Come with me," I said to Nikos. We ran down the hall back to Mr. Peary's classroom. It was empty and quiet. I peeked out the window in the door to make sure Cadence wasn't out there eavesdropping. The coast was clear. I dialed my dad's number at work, and he answered right away.

"Dad, I need your help," I said. "I have to stay and rehearse, so one of my friends is going to come by and get some stuff for the talent show tonight. Is that OK?"

"Absolutely!" Dad said with great enthusiasm. I knew the phrase "one of my friends" would get him all excited. "We'll be at the will reading this afternoon, though. We were going to go straight to the show from the lawyer's office. Can your friend come by before we go?"

"Yeah, he can come now," I said. "And then we'll meet him backstage before the show. We don't need it for the run-through."

Nikos looked like he was bursting with curiosity. He was sitting on Mr. Peary's desk with this confused smile on his face.

"Here's what we need," I said, and explained it to both Nikos and Dad. Nikos grinned and shook his head. I figured that was probably what Dad was doing on the other end of the phone, too.

"No problem, honey," Dad said.

"Don't tell Mom!" I said. "It's a surprise."

"You bet. See you at the show." He hung up.

"You got all that?" I said to Nikos. "That's really OK?"

"Yeah, sounds awesome," he said, hopping down and shouldering his backpack. "I'll be back before the show. I'll find you."

"Thanks, Nikos," I said.

I hurried back to Rory and Heidi. We decided to do our part of the run-through without the surprise. Hopefully it would still be funny when everyone saw it for real.

The auditorium was a zoo, like it is every year before the talent show. First- and second-graders were running up and down the aisles shrieking. Danny and his friends were practicing their skit at top volume. Musical instrument cases stuck out from the seats and poked people as they went by. Up onstage, a piano tuner was patiently checking the piano and trying to ignore all the noise.

We found three seats together and sat down to wait our turn. Miss Caruso came around and gave everyone a printout of the order for the show.

"I put you near the end, Ella," she said. "Since I know your performance is going to be wonderful as always."

"I'm performing with Heidi and Rory this year," I said.

"My goodness!" Miss Caruso said, smiling at them. "I had no idea you girls were musical. You're always so quiet in my class." She was being polite. Rory is rarely quiet. But usually she volunteers to crash the cymbals instead of singing, so that's probably why Miss Caruso didn't realize she could sing.

The younger grades were up first. A second-grader sang "America the Beautiful" but forgot the words halfway through and just sang the notes with nonsense syllables for the rest of the song. Two third-graders did a bunch of karate moves, although the teachers wouldn't let them pretend to fight each other. Then a couple of cute little red-headed kids did a sort of tap dance/soft shoe to an old Frank Sinatra song. When they finished, Rory clapped and went: "WOOOOOOOOO!" We looked at her in surprise.

"My stepbrother and stepsister," she explained, rolling her eyes.

"Aww, they're so cute," Heidi said.

"Oh, yeah," Rory said. "They're *adorable*. They're adorable *twenty-four hours a day*."

I couldn't tell whether she was being sarcastic or not, so I didn't say anything.

We skipped over Maggie's act because she wasn't bringing her cat until later that night. Kristal's movie turned out to be a video of her little sister that she'd made in her film class that summer. Tara's ballet performance was right before our act. She was wearing a black leotard and a flowy pink skirt and pink slippers. The beads woven all through her dark braids were pink, too. Natasha was sitting in the front row, and she clapped and yelled, "Go Tara!" when Tara came out onstage.

As I knew from being in her class all summer, Tara was amazing. She was really precise and her legs seemed a million miles long and her hands were always perfectly elegant.

"But it's not funny," Rory whispered in my ear. "Remember, the judges like funny."

"Plus she's out there by herself," Heidi said. "But we have each other!" She gave me a quick hug. I felt the hedgehogs in my stomach calm down a little. That was true. Even if the audience didn't like it, Heidi and Rory would still be on my side.

There weren't many people in the audience still paying attention when we went on. We ran through our number pretty quickly. Miss Caruso looked puzzled, but she had to hurry on to the next act. It was getting really close to six o'clock.

Finally the rehearsal was done. We were all herded into the first three rows so the audience could come in and sit down. Miss Caruso made us sit in the order we were going to perform, so I wound up right next to Tara. She fluffed out her skirt and pointed her toes and looked at me sideways.

"I like that song you're doing," she said. "It's so . . . different. For you, I mean."

"And I like your ballet piece," I said. "It's so much like the one you did last year."

She gave me a sharp look, but I kept smiling like that was supposed to be a compliment. Two can play this game, Tara Washington.

"I saw you talking to Nikos," she said. "You're not, like, *dating*, are you?"

I started to say no, but Rory leaned over and shushed us. "Miss Caruso is about to start!" she hissed in a stage whisper that was louder than most people's shouting voices.

The lights dimmed on the audience and brightened onstage. Miss Caruso made her yearly speech about how much talent there is in the school and how excited everyone is about the new year. Then she introduced the first act: a trio of first-graders showing off their "gymnastics" skills, which meant a lot of somersaults across a mat and some wobbly cartwheels.

It was cute because they were so little. I wondered if I had seemed that cute and that mediocre when I sang my first talent-show song in first grade. I hoped I was better now.

During the intermission we went backstage to get ready. Nikos was there waiting for us.

"As requested," he said, handing me a bag and patting the large covered box beside him.

"What's that, Nikos?" Tara said, sashaying up to him. She tried to peek under the blanket, but Rory swatted her away.

"You'll find out," Rory said.

"Good luck!" Nikos said. "I'll be watching!"

"Thanks, Nikos!" Tara trilled like he had been talking to her.

We waved and he went back out into the audience. Then we just had to wait. We waited through Kamala's piano performance. We waited through Danny's goofy skit about a couple of monkeys who decided to audition for a soap opera. We waited while Maggie's cat stretched and yawned and blinked and looked pretty. We waited through Tara's ballet.

And then, finally, it was our turn.

CHAPTER 16

Heidi and I carried the box out onstage and put it next to the piano while Miss Caruso was announcing us. I was wearing a pink skirt and a leather jacket I had found in my dad's closet. It said *The Smashing Mozarts* in metal studs on the back. I also had on his giant class ring from high school. I hoped it wouldn't get in the way of me playing the piano.

Heidi and Rory wore bouncy ponytails and 50s-style poodle skirts. They stood on one side of the stage, pretending to whisper and look at me. There was a murmur of curiosity from the audience. At least, I hoped it was curiosity.

I sat down at the piano as Miss Caruso stepped offstage. Putting my hands on the keys calmed me down right away. This wasn't any different from any other performance. I could do this.

I hit the first chord and started humming. That was Rory's cue.

"Is she really going out with him?" she said to Heidi.

"Well, there she is, let's ask her," said Heidi, pointing at me. She said it in kind of a rush, but you could still understand the words. They crossed the stage and came up to me. I pretended to stare dreamily into space as I played. Heidi and Rory leaned on the piano behind me.

"Betty, is that Jimmy's ring you're wearing?" Rory said to me.

"Mmm-hmm," I said, and hit the chord again.

"Gee, it must be great riding with him," Heidi said at the top of her lungs.

"Is he picking you up after school today?" Rory asked, kicking Heidi behind the piano.

"Mmm-mm," I said, shaking my head.

"By the way, where'd you meet him?" they said together.

"I met him at the candy store," I sang. "He turned around and smiled at me — you get the picture?"

"Yes, we see," they said.

"That's when I fell for —"

"The leader of the pack!" we all sang together. At the same moment, Heidi whipped the blanket off the box. Trumpet immediately poked her head out. She didn't even hesitate. She didn't care that bright lights were shining on her, or that there was an audience full of people staring at her. She knew she was born to be a star.

"AWOOOOOOOOOOOOOOOOOOOOOOOOOO-OOOOOOOOOOOOO!!!!!!" she howled, right on cue.

And right on cue, the audience started laughing. I nearly missed the next bar because they were laughing so loudly. But I stayed with it, bringing up the tempo and launching into the next verse. Heidi lifted Trumpet onto the top of the piano. Trumpet didn't miss a beat.

"AAAAAUUUUUUUUUUUUUUOOOOO-OOOOOOOOOOOOOOOOOOOOOO!!!!!!!" she warbled as I sang: "They told me he was bad — but I knew he was sad — that's why I fell for —"

"The leader of the pack!" Heidi and Rory chimed in.

This was my plan. I had found a songbook with "Leader of the Pack" in it, and I knew right away that it would be a perfect song to sing with Trumpet. Her long wild howls fit perfectly with the melodramatic song. I could sing most of it with Heidi and Rory backing me up. And we could all throw ourselves into overacting so it would be really funny.

I glanced up at Trumpet halfway through the song

and realized that someone had dressed her up, too. She had a black bandanna around her neck and tiny black leather wristbands around her front paws. She looked like a motorcycle rebel, if motorcycle rebels can also have long floppy ears and be ridiculously cute. Had Nikos done that?

We ended with Trumpet's howls fading off into silence. She lowered her head and looked around like, *That's it? I thought I got a whole fifteen minutes of fame! What's our encore?*

The audience erupted into applause. Trumpet stood up on the piano, wagging her tail. She seemed to like the applause as much as we did. She barked and barked. When I went to pick her up, she draped her front paws proudly on my shoulder and licked my face.

"Yes, you *were* fabulous," I said to her. "By far the most talented dog this stage has ever seen."

We had to come back onstage and bow a second time because the audience kept clapping and hooting for us. That had never happened to me before. I didn't remember it ever happening to anyone else at the Welcome Back Talent Show either.

"We did it!" Heidi shrieked once we were backstage again. She threw her arms around me and Trumpet. "We made it! And I didn't fall off the stage or any —" She tripped and fell backward over a pile of chairs. They all went clattering in every direction with a humongous crash.

Onstage, Cadence was playing the violin. She jumped a mile, lost her place, and had to start her piece over. The whole time she kept sending death glares our way, but we were busy helping Heidi up and trying not to laugh.

Trumpet wanted to jump down and explore all the dark corners backstage, but I kept a firm grip on her. At the end of the show, everyone went back onstage for the final bow. And then the judges came onstage, too. Principal Hansberry was one of them. She smiled right at me and Trumpet. I wondered if she liked dogs.

Heidi grabbed my elbow and held on tightly. Rory patted Trumpet's head and let her lick her hand. My heart was racing. *Don't get too excited. Stay calm*, I told myself.

"Congratulations to all our performers tonight," Principal Hansberry said into the microphone. "I am so thrilled to be joining such a wonderful school, with so many talented students. I'm really remarkably impressed."

Danny whooped loudly and Mr. Peary gave him a stern glare. Principal Hansberry went on.

"And now I am delighted to announce the winners of this year's Welcome Back Talent Show, by unanimous vote: Ella Finegold, Heidi Tyler, Rory Mason, and their surprise guest singer!" Principal Hansberry held out a bunch of flowers to us. Heidi screamed and jumped up and down. Everyone in the audience was standing up and clapping and cheering.

I was holding on to Trumpet, so Heidi and Rory stepped forward to take the flowers. We waved to the audience. I saw my mom and dad smiling. Even Isaac looked happy. I couldn't believe I'd really done it at last. We won the talent show!

"Thanks, Trumpet," I said in her ear. She wagged her tail and licked my face. It was like she was saying *Well, you were pretty good, too.*

CHAPTER 17

The auditorium was a madhouse after the talent show. About a million people came up to me to say hi to Trumpet. I didn't think I knew most of them, but they all knew my name. The first- and second-graders were really excited to pet her. Trumpet didn't mind at all. She wriggled around and licked their hands, which made them squeal and giggle. Maggie's cat hissed at us from Maggie's arms, but he seemed to be the only one who didn't like Trumpet.

Parker and Danny and Danny's sister, Rosie, came up and patted her, too. "That was awesome," Parker said. "That was maybe the funniest thing I've ever seen. Sorry," he said to Danny.

"Oh, that's OK, it's true," Danny said.

"I liked your skit, though," I said to him.

"Thanks." He grinned.

"I guess you warmed up to your dog after all," Parker said.

"Yeah, she's not so bad," I said, tickling Trumpet under her chin. Her soft brown eyes gazed up at me and her pink tongue hung out of her mouth, making her look like she was smiling.

"Hey, guess what?" Danny said. "My mom has decided we can get a dog now! I think she likes Merlin," he said to Parker. "So I'm hoping we can get something big and hairy like him."

"Not if *I* have anything to say about it!" his sister, Rosie, announced. She patted Trumpet gingerly. "*I* want something small! And cute! And adorable! *I* want a poodle! So I can dress her in cute pink out-fits and we can match!"

"Oh, no," Danny groaned. "That's all we need, a small, furry version of Rosie!"

"See you Monday," Parker said to me. "Or maybe at the dog run in the park, if you guys are ever there." He patted Trumpet's head again and they moved on to talk to Kristal.

Trumpet wriggled up my shoulder to sniff some-body behind me. Her tail wagged. I turned around, expecting my parents, but to my surprise it was Avery. He stepped back when I saw him.

"Just saying hi to your dog," he mumbled. I couldn't believe Trumpet had wagged her tail at him. Couldn't she sense that he was evil? Avery shoved his hands in his pockets. "Well, at least I didn't fall asleep this time," he said gruffly.

"I'm glad," I said, trying to sound polite and like I totally didn't care.

"Good thing your dog can sing better than you can," Avery said.

But this time, it didn't hurt my feelings. It was almost like he was trying to be funny, although he couldn't tell a joke very well. And it didn't matter what he thought. I knew everyone else had loved it.

"Thanks, Avery," I said sweetly. He rubbed his head, scowling, and then stomped off, pushing people out of his way as he went.

"Great job, Ella!" Nikos said, sliding through the crowd toward me. "You guys rocked!" Trumpet wagged her tail when she saw him. See, now there was someone she could wag her tail about. That was kind of how I felt when I saw him, too.

"Thanks for your help, Nikos. Did you give her this?" I asked, touching the bandanna.

"No, she was like that when I picked her up," Nikos said. "I had to take it off for a while so we could run around in my yard this afternoon, but I put it back on."

"That was my idea," said my dad's voice, behind

me. I turned around. Dad was grinning from ear to ear. He gave me and Trumpet a huge hug. "I figured she could use a costume, too," he said.

"I might have known you were behind this," Mom said to him.

"But it was my idea!" I said. "I found the song. Did you like it?" I asked her anxiously.

"It's not exactly what I was imagining for you," she said. "But — I loved it." Her smile was as big as Dad's. She gave me and Trumpet a hug, too. She even let Trumpet lick her ear. "It was much better than The Smashing Mozarts," she whispered.

"I *heard* that!" Dad said.

"So can we keep her?" I asked. "Please? Please please?"

"Please please please?" my dad added, giving my mom a big soulful gaze just like Trumpet's.

"YEAH! I wanna keep Trumpet!" Isaac shouted.

My mom laughed. "Now how am I supposed to argue with that?" she said. "Besides," she added, "according to the lawyers, Golda also left you a lot of money to be set aside for music school later, if you want it. So it seems wrong to take part of her gift and not the rest. I think she must have wanted you to have Trumpet for a reason."

"WOO-HOO!" Heidi shrieked in my ear, making me jump. "Sorry, I was listening in," Heidi said. "But WOO-HOO!"

I hugged Trumpet tightly and she gave my chin lots of enthusiastic licks.

"Hey," Rory said, squeezing between people to get to us. "Do you guys want to go out for pizza? My mom said she could drive us to Formosa's."

"That'd be perfect, because Trumpet could come!" Heidi said. Formosa's Pizzeria has an outside deck where they let people sit with their dogs while they're eating. I'd been there a few times with my parents, but never with a group of friends. I turned to Mom and Dad.

"Of course!" Dad said.

"Go celebrate," Mom said. "But don't stay out too late."

I felt all fizzy and happy inside. I'd won the talent show. I had two new friends — maybe even best friends. And I had the best dog in the world. Well, sort of. Hopefully no one would be singing at Formosa's.

"You want to come, too, Nikos?" Heidi said.

"I dunno," Nikos said. "Me and a bunch of girls? The other guys would never let me hear the end of it."

"Then we'll bring another guy," Rory said.

I thought of someone else who never got invited anywhere — someone who also seemed to have no friends, because of his focus on something else. "How about Pradesh?" I said. "I bet he needs a break from hearing about how amazing his sister was tonight."

"Sure," Rory said. "I'll go ask him." My mom looked even more proud of me. It was time to get out of here before she said something really embarrassing.

"Come on, Trumpet," I said. "Time to introduce you to pizza. I bet you'll like it even better than meatballs."

"Meatballs!" Mom said. "Who gave her meatballs?"

Dad and I exchanged guilty looks. "Um, nobody," I said.

"Definitely not us," Dad said. "Especially definitely not me."

"OK, 'bye, Mr. and Mrs. Finegold!" Heidi said quickly. "See you later!" She grabbed my arm and dragged me after Rory. I held up Trumpet's paw to wave to Mom and Dad and they waved back.

"This is the best night ever," Heidi said. "Man, Ella, I'm so glad you got Trumpet."

Trumpet flopped her head onto my shoulder and made a cute snoozing sound. Maybe she would sleep through the pizza-eating.

"Yeah," I said, stroking her velvety ears. "Me too."

**Buttons is a great dog ...
when she isn't getting into trouble!**

Pet Trouble
Mud-Puddle Poodle

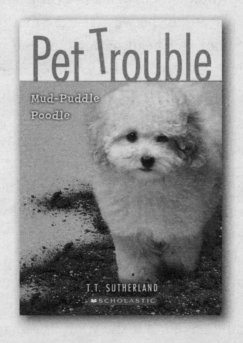

Turn the page for a sneak peek!

The puppy blinked big black eyes at us. She kind of swayed in place like she wasn't sure what to do first. Then she shook her head, crouched, and charged at Danny. Only she was too little or too sleepy to run straight, so she wobbled off course and ended up tripping over his sneaker.

"YIP!" she protested, flopping over sideways. She spotted Danny's shoelace and pounced on it like it was responsible for tripping her. She got the shoelace between her tiny teeth and dragged it backward, *grrr*ing and *snrrrf*ing and batting at it with her tiny paws.

"Hey," Danny said, trying to get it away from her. She promptly jumped on his hand. The funniest thing was that she was so tiny — she was only about the size of Danny's hand, but she went ahead and bravely attacked it anyway. But she didn't try to bite it; she had her mouth open and kept going "Arrrr arrrr" while she wrestled with his fingers.

I caught Danny hiding a smile.

The puppy still hadn't come over to say hi to me. I thought she'd sit in my lap as soon as she saw me. I thought maybe she would lick my fingers delicately a few times and then curl up and fall asleep. Instead she started running in giddy staggering circles around Danny. She kept tripping over her paws and doing little somersaults on the rug. Then she'd bounce up, blinking and looking around like she was trying to catch whoever was doing that to her.

"Come here, Princess," I said, holding out my arms to her.

"Does it have to be Princess?" Danny pleaded. "You got to pick the dog; shouldn't we get to pick her name?"

"No way!" I said. I know my brothers.

"Fuzz," suggested Miguel.

"Twinkletoes," suggested Danny.

"Marshmallow Fluff."

"Foo-Foo the Snoo."

"Señorita Fancypants!"

"Lady Snooty McSnooterfluff of the Waterford McSnooterfluffs!"

"Paperweight!"

"Kickball!"

"Danny!" I yelled.

"No, she doesn't look like a Danny," my brother said, pretending to look at the dog thoughtfully.

"Stop it!" I said. "Her name is Princess!"

"Her eyes look like little black buttons," Miguel said.

"Buttons!" Danny cried. The puppy leaped to her paws and scrambled onto Danny's lap. "See, she likes it," he said. She tried to climb his arm to get up to his face. He picked her up with both hands around her little chest and let her lick his nose. Her tail was going bananas again.

Oh, no. Maybe she *did* like the name Buttons. At least it was better than Lady McSnooterfluff or Kickball. But what about my perfect little Princess?

Mom and Belinda came back into the room. Mom saw Danny holding the puppy and gave me a thumbs-up behind his back. But that wasn't the point at all — Princess was supposed to like *me* best!

And her name was supposed to be *Princess*!

Tails of enchantment!